THE HAND-REARED
BOY
1970
1ST PRINTING

$
12.00

FOL   1/12

The Hand-Reared Boy

The Hand-Reared Boy

Brian W. Aldiss

The McCall Publishing Company

NEW YORK

The Hand-Reared Boy

ON THE ONE OCCASION THAT SISTER Traven came to tea with us we were all in confusion beforehand, and my mother was the organiser of the confusion.

She darted here and flounced there, using what she called The Light Touch to bring me or Beatrice to heel—that is, saying in a Tone of Charm something more acceptable delivered in an ordinary voice. 'No, Beatrice, dear, I think we *won't* have our ordinary serviettes, *if* you don't mind. Let's have some of the special ones, shall we, the paper ones, out of the bottom drawer of the sideboard. Or I'll get them, shall I? I'd *better* get them!'

Beatrice was not ruffled. She had been our maid for several years and was used to Mother's ways. She was now married and no longer 'living in', but she still came in the mornings, when an older married sister looked after her increasing number of children. Today she was obliging and coming in the afternoon also, as she did on these special occasions. Among the alarms of setting the tea table I watched her with interest. A rather ordinary girl—not bad!

How faithful I am, I thought. Here I'm seventeen and she's got two awful brats and must be at least twenty-five, and I still fancy her a bit!

'Darling, have you found your tie? You'd better hurry up, or she'll be here, won't she?'

'Do you think she'll mind if I haven't got my tie on, Mum, really?'

She surveyed me, smiling hard. 'She must have seen lots of little boys without ties, and without more than that, Horatio! But, after all, she is *your* guest, and I think you might try and help me just a little.'

The 'little boy' grated as much as she must have known it would.

'You wanted her round here, Mum—I didn't!'

'Sweetie, try not to be too aggravating just at this moment when I'm trying to help you and Beatrice and Ann. You know we've asked her for *your* sake. She's *your* friend, isn't she? And perhaps one day she'll ask us up to Traven House to have tea with her, and her family.'

As I sneaked upstairs to look for my tie, I passed my sister going down.

'That's all she thinks about—that Sister Traven will ask us all out to her place to tea.'

'I'm not going. I can't find my dratted shoes,'

Ann said. She was then thirteen, one of the classic shoe-losing ages.

Even when I was in my bedroom I could hear her shouting at Mother. She was far more vociferous than I.

When I was dressed, tie and all, I sat on the edge of my bed, tentatively reading a magazine. Thus Mother found me when she came upstairs.

'Ready, darling? Well, why don't you go downstairs and be prepared for your guest? Wouldn't that be nicest? I'm going to do my hair again— I must look like nothing on earth! I feel absolutely exhausted before she's even arrived. I do hope she isn't too fussy! I wish Daddy'd been able to fix the blackout properly in that room.'

'You look fine, Mum.'

'Thank you, darling.' She came nearer to me and hugged me and gave me a kiss on the cheek. 'You're a good boy, darling, a very good boy. Don't be in too much of a hurry to grow up, will you? Let me just put your tie a bit straighter. So glad you found it. I wish I'd borrowed Auntie Nell's tea service.'

'Why? Is ours broken?'

'You know how cracked and chipped it is.' She stepped back and surveyed my tie critically. 'Your collars never look right. I bet they have really lovely tea services at Traven House, don't you? You did say her father was an admiral, didn't you?'

'Rear-admiral.'

'Good. Now you go downstairs, darling, and I'll just tidy my hair and be down in a minute. And, Horatio . . .'

'Yes, Mummy?'

'Do try not to talk too Leicestershire!'

'I'll try, Mummy.'

'Watch those long 'u's then.'

Rolling the magazine and cramming one end into my pocket, I went downstairs and glumly joined my sister. We sat one either end of the sofa. She did not blame me for our present constraints, for which I was grateful. She was playing chess with herself, as Father had taught her.

Like me, Ann was munching a cachou. Mother ladled them out to us on such nerve-racking occasions as the present, when we were about to be presented to someone of importance. Perhaps they effectively heightened our charms, though I have no recollection that our breaths needed sweetening.

On these occasions Mother always took a cachou herself, as she distributed them out of a tiny cardboard box. I loved their meretricious perfumed taste, even if they were associated with nerves and straightened ties.

My mother was a tall thin woman, several inches taller than my portly father. He was ponderous where she was bird-like. His reputation (somewhat unearned) was for never giving way to excitement; she (more justly) was known to be nervous. Our doctor had recommended fresh air as a restorative for my mother's nerves and at this period of my life she was always out walking in the streets or the nearby countryside, sometimes with Ann and, less often, with me and Father lagging somewhere behind.

'You're too slow to catch a funeral!' she would call back. Father, with an elaborate display of dumb humour, would stare about, searching highway and hedgerow for sight of the hearse.

The guest whose appearance we were now so anxiously awaiting behind our perfumed defences was the nursing sister of my school, Miss Virginia Traven. I say 'my school', but by this date I had determined that school was over and done with as far as I was concerned.

Several reasons existed for this determination, chief among them that I was finding my manhood, and that this was a good time to find it. The time was mid-September 1939, when Great Britain had been at war with Nazi Germany for something under a fortnight. My older brother, Nelson, had already disappeared into the Army, and was—according to the one letter we had received from him—messing about in a barracks in Aldershot. Beatrice's husband, a husky young man who cleaned our car once a week, was reported to be training with the infantry somewhere on Salisbury Plain. My father was going through agonies of indecision about whether he should volunteer or not, and what the bank would say if he did. And I was sitting there on the sofa, picking calluses formed on my hands by the shovelling of great piles of soil on top of our air-raid shelter in the garden.

The doorbell rang. My mother cried from above, 'There she is now!'

Beatrice went to the front door. Against instructions, I followed. I wanted to get a private word in first.

Sister came lightly in, wearing her worn but tidy light tweed coat. She smiled at me with her head held slightly on one side, and quickly put her small hand into mine. Something lit in her face at the sight of mine lighting.

'Hope you won't be too bored,' I whispered. Mother was already bearing down the stairs, making little sort of preliminary tuning-up sounds. I stood back for the overture.

Meals have changed since then. They changed almost at that precise moment in time, as far as the Stubbs family was concerned. Perhaps that was the last of the rather lavish teas that my mother liked to give for her friends, sitting at the top of the table, with the teapot and its accessories by her side on a separate folding table, talking amiably to all and sundry, addressing each of her guests in turn so that none should feel left out, pausing now and then to give low-voiced instructions to Beatrice.

My poor mama! She was always happiest in the past, and this present spread was an attempt as much to stop the clock as to impress the visitor. In the recent declaration of war, boys of my age had already smelt change, and trembled; my mother's generation doubtless did the same—but their tremblings were far less pleasurable than ours.

Perhaps for this reason she decided to address Sister as if the two of them were of the same generation. I must admit now that there can have been less than ten years between them, but that gulf appeared to be infinite at the time.

Over the jelly and cream, the dainty slices of brown bread and butter, the jams in their glass dishes inside silver holders, the sponge and fruit cakes, the buns and biscuits and chocolate éclairs that were there mainly for Ann's benefit, Mother cheerfully talked of Sister's future, about which she knew even less than I.

'I must say, I think it's jolly brave of you to throw up a safe job and join the war effort! You'll have a wonderful time, lots of boy friends and admirers! Oh, I know!'

'I'm hoping to get posted to France,' said Sister.

'Lovely, what fun! Go to Paris! Such a beautiful city. Notre-Dame! The boulevards! Robert and I *love* Paris, especially in the spring . . .'

'You were only there one day, Mummy!' Ann said.

'A beautiful spring day—eat your bread-and-butter properly, Ann, and sit up straight! You'd like Paris, I know, Sister.'

'Yes, I do, very much. I have connections there.'

'Family connections, no doubt? I expect you know most of the capitals of Europe. . . . I should like to do my bit for the old country, but I'm not as free as you—three children and a husband . . .'

'You wouldn't actually call Nelson a child, would you, Mum?' I asked. 'He's in the forces and he's grown a moustache.'

Mother smiled at me and held out her hand. 'Pass your cup nicely if you'd like another cup of tea. Beatrice, I think if we could have some more hot water. . . . Nelson looks so silly with a moustache, Sister! Of course, you've never seen him. They'll soon make him shave it off. He's at Aldershot; Robert was there in the Great War. He'll always be my child if he lives to be sixty. I hope he'll do well in the Army. I believe your family are some of them in the forces, Sister, aren't they?'

A small foot kicked me under the table, and Ann made a face at me over her cup; we could almost feel Mother forcing the conversational-tone-improving word 'Admiral' to materialise in the air above the table.

'Try and drink more like a lady, Ann,' said Mother, catching the movement. 'Aren't they, Sister?'

Sister was sitting at table eating demurely, half-smiling in a way she had. She looked, I thought, rather like a dutiful young daughter, except that her face was faintly lined. Her short hair, some strands of which were quite fair, was neat and beautiful. She was so—well, you could see she was the product of upper-class breeding.

'My father and his brother were in the Navy.'

'Oh, the Navy, the senior service! And I expect they were both very successful, weren't they? Let me cut you a slice of sponge.'

'I wouldn't say successful. My father's brother, poor Uncle David, was drowned at sea.'

'You poor thing! I'm so sorry. Horatio never told me!'

'I didn't know,' I said. 'I never heard of Sister's Uncle David.'

'No, of course, you didn't,' Sister said, giving me a little secret smile. 'It was rather a tragedy. It happened in 1917. I was crazy about my uncle, although I was only a tot. He was so brave and so handsome. His ship was sunk in the Atlantic by a German U-boat. He was in the water for some incredible time, clinging to a spar. At last a British merchant naval vessel picked him up and —do you know?—he hadn't been aboard an hour before that ship was also torpedoed by a

U-boat. It went straight to the bottom, Uncle with it.'

'War's a terrible thing,' Mother said, causing a plate of cake to circulate.

'We'll soon beat the Germans,' I said. 'Their tanks are made of cardboard. The Head said so.'

There was a pause for silent patriotism and fruit cake.

'But your father's alive and well still, I hear,' Mother said.

Sister nodded. 'He's a rear-admiral. Retired, of course. Now he talks about closing down Traven House and getting back into harness, if the Admiralty will have him.'

We all smiled. Mother said, 'Rear-admiral . . . A pity the way our grand old homes have to close.'

Father had looked up Sister's home in an old *Baedeker* the previous evening, and found: '3 m. farther NE, *Traven House*, Georgian, fine Vict. orangery, once the home of Sir Francis Traven, Gov. of Massachusetts Bay, 1771–9.' We were all delighted, and wondered if Sir Francis's descendants still grew oranges there.

'Have you got any ghosts?' Ann asked. 'I'd be quite terrified! Do you have battlements, with phantom men in armour clanking about?'

Sister laughed, a very charming little display. 'No, no ghosts, no battlements.'

'But Horry told me . . .'

'Eat your cake,' I said. 'You'd be terrified of the mere thought of a ghost.'

'Don't bully her, Horatio, and do just brush your hair out of your eyes. That's better!'

'Mummy and I would love to come and see you at Traven House,' Ann said.

Our visitor looked askance. 'I'm afraid I shan't be at home much longer, Ann, otherwise I'd love to show you both round.'

The words sank deep into my heart. Although I continued to munch gloomily at the cake, I ached inside. She couldn't leave! I needed her. I loved her. She could not realise what she was doing to me or she would never go.

There were four females in the room with me. Excluding my mother, I had had sexual relations with all the others. But the need was now for Sister, entirely for Sister, only for Sister, among all the women in the world.

Should I stand up and declare my feelings? Would they laugh? What would Mother say? But Mother at this point, having poured herself a last cup of tea, was doing her party stunt and declaiming some poetry learnt as a girl:

'Old Holyrood rang merrily
That night, with wassail, and glee.
King James within his princely bower
Fêted the chiefs of Scotland's power,
Summoned to spend a passing hour.

For he had vowed that his array
Should southwards march by break of day.
Well loved that daring monarch aye
A banquet and a song.
By day a banquet and at night
A merry dance, made fast and light,
With dancers fair and costumes bright,
And *something* loud and long.
This feast outshone his revels past.
It was his biggest and his last.

'And so it goes on—I forget what comes next.
It's the court bit from Sir Walter Scott's
"Marmion". I learnt it at school. Oh, I could
spout it for hours! I tell Ann and Horatio they
ought to read more poetry. Are you a great
poetry-reader, Sister?'

Sister made some suitable reply.

After tea Ann slipped away to play in her bedroom. I hung around while Mother entertained
my guest.

'Well, darling,' she said at last, turning to me.
'Fetch Sister Traven your latest paintings. He
really does show promise.'

'I haven't done any more since I saw her last.'

Smiling, shaking of head. 'He's done several,
Sister. He's far too modest about them. I'm a great
admirer of the British artists, Gainsborough and
Hogarth, and others.' For some reason she pronounced Hogarth as if it had two g's: Hoggarth.

'It's "Hogarth", Mother. One "g".'

'I can spell Hogarth, darling. *And* pronounce it. A fine artist. We used to have a butcher called Hogarth at home, in the old days. Anyhow, Sister, it's been very good of you to take such an interest in Horatio, and to take him out as you have done. . . .'

Truer than she thought, I said to myself. I watched Sister as she rose to leave; not, if you were strictly honest, a great deal of figure. But I could discern her breasts under the jumper, and I knew how sweet they were, how pink the nipples, when you disengaged them gently from the brassière. . . . Steady, you sod, or you'll be getting a hard on. . . .

We all stood up. Mother lightly patted down a curl of hair on the back of my head, and then squeezed me affectionately.

'I tell him, if he were a girl, I'd get a slide to that piece of hair. How it infuriates me! But he's a good boy. I sometimes reproach myself that I neglect him, bless him. Yes, I've been very lucky with my children.'

'Oh, not that again, Mother! She says that to everyone, Sister. She forgets what little horrors we were.'

'I'm sure you were,' Sister said, smiling. It amazed me at the time that she was not at all put off after seeing me treated as such a kid.

'When this one cried as a child, his father got

so mad at him, he used to take him to the window and threaten to throw him out! But he was a good boy, on the whole. Well, Sister, it's been so pleasant. . . . Horatio, go and get Sister Traven's coat, where are your manners? Yes, I do hope we'll see you again soon. . . .'

As they moved to the door, I got there first, opened it, and edged myself half out before saying, 'Mother, I'll just drive down the road with Sister. There's something I want to tell her.'

'Tell her now—you've been quiet enough up to now!'

'No, it's all right. I'll tell her on the way, Mum. Then I can drop off to see William. I shan't be long.'

'Yes, all right, dear. Don't be long. Your father will be home soon.'

As Sister and I made our way down our five whitened steps and along the front path, I took her arm and led her to the car. Mother stood waving as we drove away; I hoped she had noticed my gesture.

'Let's go up by the cemetery.'

'You mustn't be long!'

It was generally quiet in the lane that ran by the side of the cemetery. She stopped in a suitable place without any mucking about. We turned and looked at each other. There was no sign on her that she had been through the ordeal I had.

We kissed each other. Not exactly a passionate kiss—I knew I would not get that kind from her at this hour of day; the passionate ones, and even the ones before the passionate ones, which were her way of testing her own mood, only materialised after dark. But certainly a loving kiss. Again I was amazed that she was not put off by Mother's attempted demonstration that I was just a kid.

'You were very nice to Mother,' I said presently.

'She was nice to me.'

Better not explore that subject! I asked her if we could drive about until it got dark. She knew what I meant.

'I must get back to Traven House, love. The family solicitor is coming over specially this evening, to sort out some of my papers. I have various bonds and other possessions, and a little not-very-valuable jewellery, that I am going to leave in his safe-keeping until the war is over.'

'God, how I wish you weren't going, Virginia!' I ran my hands over her body, but she would only stand a certain amount of that in a semi-public place. In a safe room it was another matter. Once, after dark, in the dark, she had let me undress her and I had run my hands all over her body, and then slipped a finger into her fanny and began to frig her gently. That little secret organ of hers! But there could be nothing like that on this occasion.

She had made me grow up, made me see that

there were other things than immediate satis-
factions—I would not have dared ask her to toss
me off, as I might have done with another girl;
for Virginia was teaching me immense ideas
about sexual organs—ideas that I learned only
reluctantly, ideas that went against all my early
training: showing me that love had to be there
somewhere, and that against the recurrent isola-
tion of life the hastily snatched orgasm was not
the only antidote.

Firmly, she held my hands.

'There's a war. . . . People get separated. I
learnt that in the last war, when I was younger
than you.'

'I can't bear to be separated from you, Virginia,
darling! We've only just got to know each other.'

She looked very searchingly at me, then said,
so quietly that I could hardly hear, 'You can
always write to me at my Nottingham address. I
shan't be off to London yet. . . . And, Horatio—I
must tell you. . . . You really don't know me at
all.'

I rested my head on her shoulder.

'Oh, Virginia, I want to, I want to know you
better. You're so wonderful for me, and I love
you so much.'

She never said she loved me. But she stroked
my cheeks and looked at me in what for her was
a wild sort of way.

'Virginia, I want to know you. . . .' The eternal

cry of lovers. It was eventually by getting to know
her that I lost her.

'Sweetheart, you are a child!'

'You never said that to me before. Why say it
now? I know you don't mean it as an affront—as
Mother does when she calls me a child. But I'm
sick of childhood. I'm finished with it, I hate it!
It's so *sordid*—you've showed me—Christ, *you're*
the one who has brought me out of it!'

I choked on the words. We just sat there in the
uncomfortable car, touching and looking at each
other. She never even said that she needed me,
but I had always been secure in that. I knew she
needed me; it was one of the things I understood
about her without the necessity for words.

We parted there by the bloody old cemetery,
in which my grandfather had been only recently
buried. I walked back, hands in pockets, saying
to myself over and over, 'Fuck, oh fuck, oh fuck it
all, fuck the whole shitting issue!'

And as I went along, I resolved that my childhood could be closed, after all, if I really wished
for it. Did I really wish for it? What would being
an adult entail? That was unknown. What had
being a child entailed?

All very mysterious. It had not meant a lack of
sex. I was introduced to the delights of masturbation early, and had never looked back since then.
You might say I was a hand-reared boy. Perhaps
I should have been ashamed of all that; I was not.

People pretend to be so enlightened about sex these days; they talk happily about copulation and such subjects, about adultery and homosexuality and lesbianism and abortions. Never about masturbation, though. And yet masturbation is the commonest form of sex, and tossing off the cheapest and most harmless pleasure.

Of course, as I grew older I graduated to more fashionable delights.

Shortly before I was born, my father was promoted manager of a branch of Barclays Bank Ltd. in the East Midlands. It was a small dull town then, in the early twenties, and is a large dull town now. For a reason I forget, we did not go to live in the accommodation the bank offered, but instead took over a large house on the edge of the town which had been an inn in the prosperous days, a century earlier, when the stage-coaches flourished.

One of my first memories is of the smell of beer which the floor of our living room released whenever the sun shone on it or the room was warm— ancient beer, which had soaked into the wood for decades, and could never be eradicated, however my mother set her series of maids to polishing. Could I somehow have become intoxicated by those benevolent fumes as I sprawled on the floor?

Did they have some loosening effect on my infantile moral sense? Sophisticated fellows might answer yes. But I believe the maids themselves were more to blame for my failings!

Of those maids, and in particular of Beatrice, we will speak later. First I must describe the family.

My father was a small and aloof man. He could be cold and sarcastic, to his wife as well as his children. He feared his father, my grandfather, until the day the old man died, and I believe this relationship did much to blight his pleasure in life. When my grandfather and grandmother came to stay with us, as they did all too often, my parents suffered a good deal.

My mother, on the other hand, was thin and clinging. Although far from passionate, she demanded love from her family and returned it by spasms. Terribly moody herself, the highest praise she reserved for other people was to say, 'So-and-so is always the same!' She cosseted me often, devoting much attention to me where my father devoted almost none. Yet I never doubted that he loved me deeply, just as, from a remarkably early age, I doubted whether she loved me at all.

My elder brother, Nelson, was born in 1920. He grew tall and thin and dark where I was chubby and fair. I always admired him and he tolerated me with what I regarded as marvellous

[25]

good nature. He hit me a good deal, as I suppose bigger brothers do. He loved animals and once tried to stuff a dead cat with wood shavings—his only venture into taxidermy. Nelson was a fairly clever boy, clever enough to be always slightly rebellious; he was secretly planning to become an architect, and drawing fantastic buildings, at an age when I was tamely following Father's suggestion that I should go into banking and 'work your way up'.

I was born three years after my brother, with my fists—so claimed the midwife—clenched in my eyes. 1923 was not a good year to be born. There were dock strikes in England and coal strikes in America. The French were occupying the Ruhr, Hitler was tunnelling away in Munich, like a mole under Germany's troubles. A mighty scene was already being set for my late and trivial adolescence. On the day I arrived in the world there was a severe earthquake in Japan.

My mother was always secretly frightened of men. I say 'secretly', but a mother has fewer secrets than she imagines from the young innocent tagging boredly and apparently unobservantly at her skirts. The way in which she was all friendly condescension to the tradesmen, the way she skirted the dole queues which afflicted the Midlands—and perhaps much more subtly the way all her appeals and coquetry towards Father were framed—spoke of her terror of the male.

Although both her parents were dead long before I arrived howling on the scene, they had been a formidable couple by all accounts; her father, whose old farm we sometimes drove past in our tiny black car, had been a tyrant of the Victorian school. No doubt he, and the stern nonsenses with which he could fill a small girl's head, were sufficient to give her a scare for life.

Marriages (I was told as a kid) are made in heaven. In fact, they seem to be made in a tiny dim, shuttered, undiscovered room in the brain, where some fiendishly clever little hunchback of a genius sees to it that we get the marriage partner we *really* want, whatever we think we want, and however we rail against his choice later.

I believe that, much though my mother suffered from my father's coldness and his sarcastic tongue, she chose him because he was aloof and did not 'trouble her too much'.

Since I do not go far with the psycho-analysts, I'd better drop that line of reasoning. It makes sense to try to make sense of our parents; it is part of the process of understanding ourselves. As far as Freud helps common sense, he is welcome. I suppose he might have agreed that, for whatsoever reason, my mother was happier in the company of her own sex.

For that reason she badly wanted a little girl. If Nelson was a disappointment, Horatio was a greater. Not being a maths wizard, she must have

felt that the chances of the second baby being a
girl were twice as great as the first time. My
father, who, as a banker, could no doubt have
enlightened her on that simple excursion into the
realm of probability theory, characteristically did
not. Mother went into what was euphemistically
termed 'a nervous breakdown' and took several
months to recover. Perhaps it was in some sort of
revenge for that that they called me by the unfor-
tunate Christian name I bear; or perhaps, had I
been a girl, they had been intending to christen
me Emma; when my father read a book it was
about British heroes—preferably Nelson.

Anyhow, the mother would not look at the new
baby, or was advised by the family medico not to
look at the new baby. A wet nurse was found for
the new baby, and he went to stay in her house
for the first two months of his existence.

Was it that early exile that tipped the sexual
scales? I ask myself . . . . but no longer very
fervently!

Legend has it that my father came every evening after the bank closed to inspect his second son
and to see that the wet nurse was looking after
him. The action sounds hardly characteristic of
Father, although the story sounds characteristic of
Mother's tales.

What she suffered then goes unrecorded—like
most suffering. She could never afterwards entirely
decide on her behaviour towards me. Should she

blame me because she 'nearly died' on my arrival? Or should she make it up to me because I had been sent away at once? She never solved the problem.

A partial solution arrived four years after I was born. In the summer months of 1927 she achieved her long-awaited daughter. Caroline Adelaide Ann Stubbs opened her eyes upon the world, and found it good. She also found it good that a devoted mother awaited her every behest.

The birth of Ann, as the baby was called in the family, brought a measure of happiness to us. We were glad that Mother was glad. Nor was this particularly unselfish; it gave Father more peace, and it gave Nelson and me the chance to play with less supervision. I believe we really loved Ann, almost as much as Mother demanded we should. True, my brother did drop her once while carrying her round the garden, but I re-call the sincerity of his penitence after, which had nothing to do with Mother's tears or Father's chastisement!

Mother's success with Ann went to her head— or womb, rather. Two years later she bore another little girl, but this baby was still-born.

I recall poignantly the news of its arrival. One of the maids was keeping Nelson and me amused; she kept running out of the room and coming back, telling us, 'You'll hear it cry presently! It's coming now!' I remember leaving our toys and going to kneel on the wooden window seat; I stared through the panels of yellow semi-frosted glass that flanked our windows and wondered what it felt like to be a child that as yet was no-where—listening eagerly for its cry and hearing instead a cuckoo, asking myself if there was a connection between mysterious bird and myster-ious baby. Then Father came and told us—he took our hands—that the baby was dead and Mummy was very sad.

'It would have been a little sister for you,' he said. 'But God took her away again at the last moment.'

After that we were more devoted than ever to Ann. Neither Nelson nor I would have put it past God to take her too.

Our little town boasted one superior kinder-garten, run by a Miss Matilda Unwin, and to this I was sent at the age of five. Nelson was almost ready to leave and go on to grammar school.

Kindergarten was satisfactory enough. We bullied and were bullied, but nothing very terrible. I was immediately attracted to several of the girls and, although most of this attraction was entirely undeclared, it was generally recipro-cated in some degree, which contributed considerably to the pleasures of school, since seats were scarce in the youngest form and we had to sit two at a desk. So I was able to cuddle against Sheila, in her lovely golden-brown cord dress, which reminded me of wallflowers. It had a white lace collar, and white socks went with it. Her legs were pretty, but I believe I loved her only on the days when she wore that fetching little dress.

I was continuously fond of Sonia, who had attractively short-cropped fair hair. She was a tough and adventurous little girl and we used to play together out of school. At one time we planned to marry, but then she was sick in class, right—splash!—into her desk, and I turned my affections elsewhere.

Even in those days, just like adults, we thought of little but sex, although it took diffuse and childish forms. We invented a lovely game to play in the playground: Farmers and Cows, it was called.

With our heels, we scraped outlines for sheds in the playground gravel. And with sure instinct the boys were the cows and the girls were farmers or dairymaids, coming to milk the cows. This meant they had to give a really good squeeze and feel of our tiny genitals. It was the best game we ever invented!

Innocent fool that I was, I ran home and told my mother about it. She flew into a terrible fright, trotting round the room and seizing up

Ann before her to cuddle—whether to protect the child or herself, I don't know. I was forbidden to play Farmers and Cows again.

But the old serpent of sexuality was rampant on the playground now. The girls naturally wished to know more about the strange udders of their cows. Behind Miss Unwin's house, beside the water-butt, by the tatty privet hedge, I unbuttoned my fly-buttons and showed my rosy little wee-wee to Sheila and Hilda.

They were interested but sceptical. Hilda, darling girl, reached out and touched it and said it was nice. Sheila was more cautious. Already our grown-up selves were foreshadowed there.

The next picture I have is of a slight advance. The water-butt again, scene of happiness and depravity. Sheila and Hilda there again, and a smaller girl, name forgotten. Again I open my trousers and exhibit. Again they stare, with none of the maidenly modesty that will afflict them in a very few years.

Hilda and the little girl look very closely, getting in each other's way. Sheila stands back, half-leaning against the wall.

'It's nice,' says the small girl. She makes no attempt to touch. 'You can come and play in my garden after school, if you like.'

She lifts up her dress and takes her knickers down; Hilda follows suit. Both show me what they have, and the little girl giggles a lot and flaps her skirt up and down. I concentrate on Hilda's thing. It looks pretty and chubby. Her stomach and thighs are pleasant to me.

I say to Sheila, 'Let me see yours too.'

'Some other time,' she says, lolling from side to side, smiling into the distance, confident possibly that I would enjoy what she kept concealed. As far as I recall, she never did show me.

After school Hilda and I decided that we would go into the little girl's garden and play, the assumption being that we could then have a better look at each other. But the little girl was met at the school gates by a nanny and led away firmly by the hand, while we were shoved away.

Time went by, the endless congealed time of children and lunatics. Basically, cricket and Red Indians interested me more than female wee-wees. They seemed to possess more potential in those days.

The slump was on. Father went about with a long face, predicting that the bank would have to close. 'Money has dried up,' he said. Money has dried up—a marvellous phrase! I pictured it golden, damp, congealed, like beaches as the tide leaves them.

We were seeing something of beaches at this time. Taking advantage of a customer's bankruptcy, my father bought from him a small bungalow on the North Norfolk coast. We used to drive there for summer weekends—a long boring drive that grew interesting only when we got through Spalding and King's Lynn and could smell the sea. The bungalow was on the dunes just outside Hunstanton. The tide went out for miles, leaving all that congealed money, and I never got over the wonder of it.

The sea air was supposed to 'do me good'. I suffered much from bilious attacks at the time, greatly to the bafflement of our family doctor and my parents. Nelson called me a dirty beast, but I was always scrupulous about never being sick anywhere but in the right place.

It is clear enough to me now what ailed me. I was emotionally upset by my mother.

She was no disciplinarian. Father would take a stick to Nelson and me when we were naughty; it was a painful punishment that left no after-effects —only Father's habit of insisting I shook hands with him directly afterwards, as if to absolve himself from guilt, faintly annoyed me. But Mother's way of inducing goodness into us was altogether more deadly. She threatened that she would not love us any more, and that she would run away from home, taking Ann with her.

Perhaps such threats would mean nothing to an insensitive child, if there is such a thing. To me, who had experienced separation from my mother at birth, they loomed enormous. I was frequently sick because that would keep Mother at home; she pampered me marvellously when I was ill in bed. (At the time, of course, I had no inkling of my own thought processes.)

My mother was capable of actually carrying out her threats. On one occasion, when Nelson and I had done something of which she did not approve, she put Ann into her coat, hat, and leggings, stuffed her in the push-chair, and was off. We had the terrible mortification of seeing her from our bedroom windows, heading for the market place, Ann howling with apprehension as she went. If my memory serves, this was the last occasion on which I saw Nelson cry. We cuddled together against the bed and wept, 'She'll never come back! We must try to be better boys!'

No doubt Mother's treatment of us had much to do with her mysterious nerves, which the seaside was expected to alleviate. Sometimes, Grandfather and Grandmother came down with us for the day, to look after the children while Mother went for one of her walks along the beach. In covert misery I used to watch her tall figure dwindle in the perspectives of the shore, wondering whether she meant to return, or whether something mysterious and terrible would happen to her as soon as she was out of my sight.

Sometimes she would take one of these seashore walks with 'Uncle' Jim. Uncle Jim Anderson was a smiling man with cold red hands who made rare and ambiguous intrusions into our family life. He and Father were always very hearty with each other. When Uncle Jim appeared at our bungalow he would bring amazing things to eat at picnics—game pies and pineapples, I remember—and was welcome on that account. But he would also accompany Mother on her long walks; then Nelson and I became strangely uneasy and refused to swim, even when Grandfather shouted at us.

'Do you think he and Mum are up to something?' Nelson asked. We suspected they were, although we had not the vaguest idea what people did when they were up to something.

When Nelson was going to grammar school he became more remote from me. In my own little animal world I formed a tentative pact with Ann. Although Mother mothered her vigorously, Ann was by no means her slave, as I felt I would have been had I received such smothering kindness. Ann reserved her independence. This meant that she was not entirely a reliable ally; anything I did which she disliked was reported at once, and loudly, to Mother. Yet she plotted against Mother in her own right and, of us three children, she was the most subversive. She was a clever and inventive child, and together we used to stray far from home over the common. Once we saw an old tramp take his trousers down and shit under a gorse bush, which embarrassed us both greatly.

We invented a fascinating and perilous game in the back garden. It began, I believe, after Mother took us all to the circus in Nottingham and we had seen some acrobats performing.

Ann and I were tightrope-walkers. The clothes-line lay on the lawn, and we walked along it, pretending to sway perilously and occasionally fall off. Later we acquired a length of thick rope. With Nelson's aid, this was stretched tightly between two apple trees, a foot or so above the ground. Ann and I soon learnt to walk along this with our shoes off, so that we were able to raise the height of the rope.

At its most developed, this game became quite professional.

The rope was stretched from the corner of the garden shed to our biggest apple tree, perhaps a yard above the ground. Sometimes we were in the jungle, escaping from wild animals, but more often we were kings, tightrope-walking above England; we could have as much of it as we could walk over without falling off. This must have presaged a later and more megalomanic game to be mentioned in due course.

Despite the gloomy predictions of our parents, I cannot recall that Ann and I ever hurt ourselves at this game, except on the final occasion we played it. We had tied one end of the rope to a vertical drainpipe running down the side of the

shed; the drainpipe came away from the brickwork when I was on the rope. Falling, I did no
more than graze a knee.

The craze was over, just another of the crazes
of childhood, like marbles or hoops. I cannot
recall ever trying to tightrope-walk again. Other
attractions claimed me; among them was Hilda.

In my last year at the kindergarten I was in
love with Hilda. She was my age, pretty and
slender, with curly brown hair. Her father was
a hairdresser; he also ran the local amateur
dramatics group with his wife. The theatrical
streak lay in Hilda also. She would tease me, but
captivatingly, and dance for me. Her mother was
always buying her pretty dresses, of which I
thoroughly approved.

Hilda and I spent a lot of time together. She
cured me of my final Red Indian craze. We used
to go and play with a pallid boy-cousin of hers,
Ronnie, because Ronnie lived in a huge house
with lots of agreeably derelict outbuildings. We
could always scare Ronnie by pretending we had
seen a ghost in the stables. On the other hand,
Ronnie could scare *us* by saying he saw ghosts in
the house. I've often wondered about this inter-
changeability of roles, which occurs in adult life
too, for our characters are by no means as fixed
as we like to think. In this particular case there
was an immediate explanation: Hilda and I
knew the stables were not haunted, but we sus-

pected the house was, and were easily alarmed by anything that tended to confirm that suspicion. Ronnie, knowing the house to be haunted, would naturally expect ghosts in the outbuildings.

But I have seen boys at school, miserably bullied one term, turn into tough little bullies the next; and the sloppiest soldiers, given a stripe, are transformed into bull-shitting corporals. Cowards turn into heroes, heroes into cowards, according to circumstance rather than nature.

Hilda and I turned into lovers. We used to kiss each other a lot, though I never kissed her as much as I wished. Kissing her was absolute delight; I never wished for anything better. When we had scared Ronnie we would walk in the dead passages or climb into the old lofts, playing our tiny games. Once, I was taken to see her perform on the stage. She sang two songs: 'An Apple for the Teacher' and 'Little Man, You've Had a Busy Day' (only she sang, 'Little Girl, You've Had a Busy Day'), and I clapped furiously.

We inspected each other's bodies and rather politely kissed each other's behinds. The look of her body was a delight to me. But we did not know what to do except look. I stood against her, touching her, but I believe that was only once or twice. We used to watch each other pee.

It was Margaret Randall, however, who gave me my first erection.

Miss Unwin divided her flock into Little 'Uns

[39]

and Big 'Uns, or Little Unwins and Big Unwins, as we said. The Big 'Uns went into an upstairs classroom. Margaret Randall was one of the biggest of the Big 'Uns, due to leave at the end of term; I myself had only a couple of terms to go. On this momentous occasion, when Miss Unwin was momentarily out of the room, Margaret locked the door of the classroom, jumped on to the table, called to us all to gather round, and began stripping off her clothes.

Children take things for granted. We enjoyed the show without being surprised. Margaret had an attractive face, with big blue eyes and long eyelashes. A nice girl, good with the Little 'Uns. As she pulled her knickers off, we saw with delight —surprised perhaps at the inevitability of it!— the crisp black hair that seemed to curl from between her legs.

She danced seductively on the table, making her small breasts bounce. I was entranced; I believe we all were. As she leaned backwards, legs open, I saw the pink inner lining of her vagina. For the first time I fully realised the thing would open, and my flesh gave a flip of delight. The wee-wee was giving place to the penis.

There was furious hammering at the door as Miss Unwin tried to get into the classroom and failed. Margaret gave one final waggle of her hips, jumped off the table and climbed back into her clothes. I forget what explanation was offered to the headmistress; I was far too preoccupied with what had happened.

Margaret Randall left at the end of term. Soon I also left and went to the grammar school, an old and crumbling building where lessons at first came very hard. Nelson was far above me in the school and embarrassed by having his kid brother hanging about waiting for him every afternoon. He thumped me a good bit, to prove to his pals that he was no cissy. I was punched in the stomach by a boy called Ian Barrett, whom I thenceforth feared and loathed.

Worse was in store. Hilda had to have her adenoids and tonsils out. After the operation she became rather fat. She went to a new school and became terribly lady-like. Her cousin Ronnie, too, was becoming less chicken-hearted, and insisted on looking when Hilda undressed. I was cross about this, particularly as Hilda obliged for him with no sign of ill will. I remember he once asked me to take my trousers down for him. I refused.

So I ceased actively to love Hilda. We had grown apart.

At home, things were no better or worse. I still hoped that my mother might grow to love me. The more she said she did, the more I doubted it.

There was reason. Mother had many acquaintances with whom she was always taking tea or playing whist, including Molly Hadfield, whose husband owned the town's biggest grocery. Before meeting Molly, Mother would be all complaints about her and how awful she was. As soon as they met, Mother was sweet as pie—just as she was with me when in good humour—and paying Molly all sorts of compliments. Molly, liking this treatment, would respond with all the scandal. I cannot remember a word she said, being merely a captive audience and bored with the whole visit. After she had gone, Mother would instantly tell whoever was about—Ann or me, if nobody else was there—just what a nasty, back-biting, insincere little piece-of-goods Molly Hadfield was. Nelson, Ann, and I heard this so often, and winced when Mother went into her charm act before other people. She did it to the end of her days. It never ceased to be painful to me.

Home-life, however, was not all bad. A child's life, in any case, is more compartmented than an adult's. My bilious attacks were now fading out, giving way to fits of anger, which frightened me almost as much as they did everyone else. I was regarded as 'a difficult child', and my father became even more distant than before (which probably intensified the anger fits if they were, as one might suppose, signals for help). Poor Ann had to bear most of the brunt of these fits—most, that is, after the furniture—but this in no way altered our somewhat sporadic affection for each other.

We had a new game in which Nelson occasionally joined. We had found a huge gold-mine in India (my grandfather had spent several years in India) and, with its contents, Ann and I had bought England and shipped it somewhere else. I'm not quite sure *where*, and wasn't at the time; the details were deliberately left vague. Everyone in England was on our side and adored us. Everyone else in the world was against us, and kept trying to steal the country from us. We were so famous and so loved that motion-picture cameras were trained on us all the time, even when we went to the lavatory; these films were rushed to cinemas all over England, to appease the population, who sat in the cinemas most of the time, gloating over our *niceness* in the dark, cheering when we beat off the crooks or farted or waved to the cameras. (A new cinema had just opened in town.)

I was getting good at cricket too. Every game, I was playing for England, nothing less.

God knows to what lengths this self-aggrandisement might have gone. But we found another game, a sex game.

Nelson was thirteen when he got me in the garden and showed me how to masturbate. It was extremely interesting. Later, he showed me again in the bedroom, where we could get a good look. Although I had seen his penis for years, without thinking it of any particular account, I now observed how well it had developed. He urged me to try rubbing my prick; with the promise of similar development, I tried there and then, with no effect. Was the sensation even pleasurable? I forget.

Memory is an elusive thing. It stores episodes well, but misses out intervening passages of time. Some months must have passed before I was tempted to try again. With Nelson's help I was then more successful.

This episode took place in Ann's bedroom, which doubled as playroom, Ann being out at the time.

Nelson's contribution to our England game was to build huge and strange edifices out of Ann's and our old building bricks. The fantasy was that we inhabited these palaces. They were his first flights as an architect, elaborate structures as high as Ann, which incorporated old boxes and bits of toys; sometimes they had Ann's dolls imprisoned in their rooms and staring helplessly out of windows. When we had built one of these fine erections between us we went on to the wanking game. He brought his penis out, made it stand, and made me produce mine. He worked at it, and it also became erect.

What excitement and delight!

At once I wanted to bring Ann in on the new game. Nelson was more cautious, recalling that she 'will only tell Mum'.

Ann did not tell Mum, however. She enjoyed the game too much. I introduced the idea rather carefully, when we were both getting dressed one Saturday morning and running between each other's bedrooms. Producing the mystery object from my pyjamas, I held it in my hand and invited her inspection; it gave her the traditional pleasure females derive from the sight.

We persevered. Soon it would stir and rise at her touch. The idea of rubbing it came naturally to her.

Life also had its less enjoyable side. I was involved in fights at school, mainly desultory punch-ups on the way home in the afternoon. One day, however, I again fell foul of Ian Barrett. He ganged up on me with a crony of his, jostling me in the lane behind the school. I hit him and he hit me back, on the nose. I lost my temper in the same wild way I did at home. I waded into him, swiping wildly, entirely out of control. Barrett's crony ran for it. At first, Barrett punched back, but I was too enraged to be stopped by pain. He fell over. I kicked him and then fell on him, still punching, yelling, and snivelling.

A group of boys came up and dragged me off, staring at me in awe. Barrett just lay there.

I ran away, half-believing I had killed Barrett.

My nose was bleeding. The blood was all over my clothes. I did not dare to go home in that state: Mother would have deserted us for good and all. Miserably, I slunk along side streets full of hostile houses and windows, crossed the railway, and made my way over the common to a pond on which we used to slide when it was ice-covered in winter. It was the only place I could think of where I might wash unseen.

As I cleaned up, shame came over me. That Barrett was bigger than I, and older, I could not accept as an excuse. I was also sorry for myself, feeling I ought to be able to run home to sympathetic and even admiring parents. Wretchedness overcame me as I mopped my clothes, knees, and face. Yet a saving streak of humbug allowed me also to glory in my wretchedness.

Cold and dread finally drove me home, bespattered now with mud as well as blood. Mother was frantic with worry. I was sent straight up to my room, told to await my father. Ann and Nelson stared at me as I stumped upstairs. Neither dared even wink at me.

When my bedroom door opened, it was Beatrice, the maid. She had brought me a slice of cherry cake in her hand. I grabbed it, and the door quickly shut again. I was too miserable to eat the cake, and hid it under my pillow.

When Father came up he looked very stern, closing the door behind him and standing against it as if he were facing a firing squad.

'Mr. Barrett phoned me. Ian ran straight home and told him what you have been up to, fighting like a common little guttersnipe. Mr. Barrett was furious.'

'He hit me first, Dad!' And the little sniveller had blabbed! But at least he was not dead, as I had feared.

'That's no excuse. Mr. Barrett was furious. You have got to get cleaned up and then go round and apologise to him, and to Ian.'

'I won't! I won't! And you aren't going to make me!'

'We'll see about that, my boy!'

Time-honoured exchanges! But my father did not see about it. Even as I defied him, I comprehended that inwardly he was on my side. Mr. Barrett might have alarmed him, but I had won his sympathy.

Relenting slightly, he said, 'Well, let's get you cleaned up first. You are in a mess! Look at your clothes!'

I started shivering and blubbering. He helped me out of my filthy little suit and came with me to the bathroom to supervise a general sponging-down. We discovered several cuts and bruises under the dirt. On to these my father dabbed iodine—an ordeal in its own right.

Eventually I was allowed downstairs, feeling very small. My mother was taken to one side and spoken to, while Nelson and Ann gazed at me.

'You really bashed old Barrett up,' Nelson said.

'Yeh.'

[47]

I could hardly eat high tea. But nothing more was said about going round and apologising to Barrett or his horrible father.

My world seemed greatly to have changed. Curiously enough, at home and at school, things went on as ever. Nobody realised how gravely I had scared myself by completely losing control of my emotions.

Nelson and I now held regular wanking sessions. Soon we took it as a matter of course that Ann should be present. She insisted on being present, threatening to make a fuss if we would not have her—for I had not long been able to resist telling her that Nelson had an even bigger one than I.

At first she was content to watch. Later she began to insist on doing it to one or other of us. We had to admit that this was more enjoyable than doing it to ourselves.

She also did it to us both at the same time, a penis in both hands, but this seemed rather clumsy. Although it was scarcely true to say that we looked on what we were doing as wrong, we certainly took good care that our parents did not discover us at it.

Ann had a nasty school friend called Rosemary. She asked us once if Rosemary could attend a

session—'not touching, just looking'—but Nelson
and I refused; we disliked Rosemary. Nelson told
Ann that some boys looked different because they
had skin over the ends of their cocks; there were
boys at school like that. She begged Nelson to
bring someone of that kind home, so that she
'could have a go with it'. Nelson told me later
that he had approached a boy he knew and
suggested it, but the boy refused.

This ur-sex with our sister was entirely a one-
way transaction. We took it for granted that she
had no instrument, and there was an end to it;
she seemed to labour under the same delusion.
Neither Nelson nor I, to my recollection, ever
tried to examine her crack, although we both
had enough knowledge by then to grasp that
that crack represented a decided presence
and not just an absence. But we weren't interested.

No doubt our own little cocks seemed far more
fascinating than anything Ann could offer, for at
this age we were passing through a proto-homo-
sexual phase often noticeable in boys. But I
believe there was something more to it than that:
the question of personality entered, personality
of which sex is only a part. Children respond instinctively to each other's characters, often in a
way baffling to adults, who will cry plaintively,
'But Jimmy's such a nice little boy, dear!', or 'I
do wish you could find a better playmate than

Freddie!', in their inability to see the real nature of Jimmy and Freddie.

For all the frequent sex-play between Nelson, Ann, and me, our relationships were in fact formal and carefully guarded beyond a certain limit—unlike the relationship between Hilda and me; Hilda and I loved each other, as far as our immature personalities were capable of it; we were intimates.

Hilda apart (and by now she was well on her way to plumpness and her new school manners), sex in these days had little to do with love or affection; curiosity was the basis of it.

Roaming through the fields with a couple of my pals one day, and stopping for a pee, I saw that one of them had the other kind of prick, with skin. When we were alone I asked him to let me have a look at it.

He brought it out willingly. It seemed a very strange object, somewhat long and pale, with the skin coming right over the red knob and ending pink and pursed almost like the bud of a small flower. He let me finger it. When I rubbed it a bit for him, nothing happened. I believe I asked him if it would open and he said no.

That time of life is a curious mixture of know-ingness and complete ignorance. In the summer term I played in the school cricket team, and gained a reputation as a fast bowler. We were all sitting behind the pavilion, smoking—sharing two fags between the group of us—when one of the bigger boys, Peter Adamson, a good bat, told us that he knew where babies came from. The Adamsons' maid had told him. He said that they came from ladies' cracks and that, before they came out, pricks had to be stuck up the crack.

The notion struck us as both repulsive and unlikely. Peter insisted that the maid had shown him how it was done, demonstrating with a finger up her own crack.

Infuriated by his persistence in such a lie—such a disturbing lie!—we seized him and beat him on the behind with his own bat!

Peter's preposterous tale lingered in my mind. So did my interest in uncircumcised penises. When a big plump boy called William offered to show me his, I was eager. William, by his own account, 'flapped himself', as he called it, every night. His penis felt pulpy and peculiar, and was covered by a very thick skin, which I touched. It became erect in my grasp and he let me draw the skin back, to reveal his glistening knob brightly coloured. I wanked him for some while until he shuddered and groaned and gasped and cried 'Faster!' to me.

That was exciting. Although I did not greatly like William, his home was fairly near ours, and so we returned from school in the same direction. Just out of our way stood an old semi-derelict farm which the farmer had half-converted into a filling station. One of those gaunt old petrol pumps of the thirties stood there, and old broken cars, and a shiny metal sign advertising 'Pratt's High Test'—a brand of petrol. William got me into the back of these premises through a hole in the hedge, and we there investigated each other.

I did not much like his holding my penis. But I had the notion, before his grew too large, of inserting my knob under his foreskin. In this unusual position we proceeded to wank ourselves off. It excited me as much as it did William. Eventually he broke loose, rubbing himself briskly and crying 'Here it comes!' I was mystified, and not unmoved, by my first glimpse of anyone undergoing orgasm.

No sense existed then of urgency, or of the need to follow up one thing with another, such as one feels as an adult. The phenomena of life were isolated. There were so many phenomena; it had to be left to chance to see which connected to which.

For all that, my interest in sex was growing. I confided in neither Nelson nor Ann about my activities with William, perhaps because they disturbed me too much. It was the contortions he went into, as well as the mystery of that extra piece of skin. He rubbed me also, on two occasions—enjoyable for me, but he was annoyed that 'nothing happened' to me, and after the second occasion I would not let him do it again, though

I continued to manipulate his foreskin whenever the idea entered our heads. Each time he went shuddering off into climaxes I could not understand.

If this sounds inconclusive it was inconclusive in a deeper sense. I knew from my limited experience that sex was pleasurable; I could not know that it was more pleasurable than I had experienced. Of orgasms, I comprehended nothing. William's pleasurable writhings had no meaning; perhaps I regarded them as a kind of affectation on his part, a facet of his rather unpleasing character.

This record is predominantly sexual in its emphasis. In my life, and more especially in my childhood, it was not so. This truth, while it affects every page, cannot be repeated on every page.

Ann's interest in sexual organs was as great as mine. She had not abandoned her plan for introducing her nasty school friend to our sessions.

Rosemary's nastiness lay mainly in the eye of the beholder. She wore plaits with ribbons in and was somewhat pallid, but that was the extent of what Nelson and I had against her. At this period I was still undergoing my 'girls are soppy' phase. (Ann, as a sister, did not come within the girl category.)

Because her hold over me was firmer than her hold over Nelson, Ann managed to get me alone with her and Rosemary in her bedroom.

'Show Rosemary your cock,' she said. There was a lack of finesse in those days!

I brought it out, cradling it protectively in my open palm while the girls inspected it. Rosemary was an only child; she had probably never seen anything like it before. Although I was happy to assist in her education, it was irritating to submit to investigation. The two girls had been colouring some pictures. With a crayon, Rosemary prodded my prick, trying to make it turn over.

'I'll show you how to work it. Watch me make it grow big!' Ann said. Kneeling down by me, she cradled and stroked my prick as if it were one of her guinea pigs. She whispered to it encouragingly, tickling and rubbing it underneath, enticing it, while Rosemary awaited the miracle. Under her stony stare, the pet would not come to life, and I slid it back into my trousers.

Only a few days after, Rosemary was playing in the house when I came home. I ran up to my bedroom to dodge her. She followed me in and said, 'Can I get it out?'

'Get what out?'

'You know—your thing. Your little plonk. Please!'

'You don't like it,' I said, sulkily.

'I *do* like it. Really!'

'I suppose you can, then.' I wasn't keen for her to do so, but it seemed uncivil to refuse. The parents had been careful to instil rules of hospitality in us.

I stood there while she clumsily unbuttoned my flies, looking down at her head and her plaits. She had a neat white parting, unexpectedly pleasing. Amateurishly, she felt in my trousers, fumbled gently to grope her way into my pants. Sensing her approach, my prick flipped up to attention.

She drew it forth. 'It's awfully big today!'

Admiringly, she traced round the rim of the glans penis with a finger.

'You can rub it if you like,' I said loftily. I showed her how to do it. She started, but Ann called her, and she ran away.

When she had gone I remembered how her parting had looked, and wished I had asked her to show me her crack. It never occurred to me to ask her another time.

Life went on. Nelson was now working hard for exams. He wore spectacles and was more remote from us. For all that, our wanking sessions were still held intermittently, more secretively; Nelson began to prefer Ann not to attend. He said it was 'bad for her'.

He crept into my bedroom one morning and said, 'Horace, boy, I can come!' Opening his pyjamas, he showed me his penis, hanging large and limp; he had just masturbated. Above the root of it, downy hair was growing: not much of it, but decidedly hair! I had heard that what we then called spunk came out of the ends of full-grown penises.

'Show me!' I said. He began rubbing his organ, pressing it back and forth with his fingers until it struggled into an erect position. Then I took over from him, kneeling up on the bed to get at it properly.

'Bathroom's free!' my father called, thumping on my door as he passed.

'Just coming!' I shouted back. Nelson jerked away at the sound of Father's voice, but I grabbed hold of his prick and worked away excitedly, rubbing my own with my free hand.

'Oh, here it comes!' Nelson gasped, pressing his palms against his thighs. I redoubled my efforts with both hands. Bubbles appeared on the end of his prick, quite a few, nothing more.

'There was more stuff last time,' he said—but neither of us was disappointed. This was the first time I realised that sexual activity had a positive visible climax. Although I continued to rub myself when Nelson had left the room, nothing similar happened to me.

Over these years we children were left surprisingly much to our own devices, once we were over the stage when Mother took Ann out for a walk every afternoon. She returned to a round of committees and afternoon teas and card games while the maids saw Ann to and from school. Father was down in the bank, often returning only when it was time for us to go to bed.

The maids had almost as much freedom in the afternoon as we had. For most of my childhood we had a maid living in, another maid who was at the house all day, and a washer-woman and boot-boy who came only in the mornings. There was also a nurse-maid while Mother was slowly recovering from her still-born child. The maids wore uniform, which included little lace caps and aprons. If it all sounds very Victorian, the English provinces in the thirties were still labouring under the shadow of the old queen. My grandmother was still washing her painted wooden venetian blinds, her anti-macassars, and her bead-curtain while Hitler's divisions were entering Prague.

If maids also feature largely in Victorian sexual anecdotes, well, such eminence was surely justified. Lucky the son whose family boasted a nice maid.

Beatrice was certainly interested in the whole matter of sex—painfully interested, one might say. At one time I had been rather violently interested in Beatrice. The maids shared a separate lavatory with the boot-boy, in the back

of the house, next to the scullery and the boot-
hole. I managed to dash in there several times
and catch Beatrice with her knickers down,
peeing. She was always furious, and the final
crushing threat to 'tell the Missus' cured me of
the habit.

That episode was a couple of years past by the
time she caught me tossing myself off.

Our Beatrice was a bit of a spy. She was a quiet
girl, with pleasant and rather flat features, small-
built, and with a crop of brown hair which was
generally worn done up in a bun. She put her
quiet habits to good effect by creeping up on us
unawares. Thus it was that she overheard Ann
talking to Rosemary about what Nelson and I
did together. She then kept watch to see what
happened.

In the afternoons when Mother was out I was
careless. This particular afternoon was in the
summer, just before school broke up. I had been
swimming with some other boys, and came back
to find the house deserted, although I could hear
Beatrice in the kitchen preparing tea. I went up
into my bedroom and, without even bothering
to shut the door properly, flung off my school
uniform to change into other clothes.

Catching sight of myself in the long wardrobe
mirror, I began to posture lewdly at myself. I
stood on my hands and let my penis dangle down
my stomach. I stuffed it between my legs and

pretended I was looking at a girl. I tried to push it into a thin-necked vase. I embraced the mirror.

The object of my attentions raised its head. I started to rub it, drew up a chair and sat there, leisurely stroking it and gazing at it admiringly in the mirror, wondering why my parents had seen fit to rob me of my rightful foreskin.

When my prick was as stiff as a little rod, a noise made me turn my head. There stood Beatrice, looking mighty peculiar, her face telling me at once that she had been watching.

Everything seemed to happen in slow motion.

'I'll tell your mother, you doing that to yourself!' she exclaimed.

She came forward, almost despite herself. I shut my legs, stood up, put my hands over my weapon, and faced her, aghast, unable to say anything. The room seemed to be full of silence.

'I'll tell your mother!'

She pulled my hands away. My prick was still standing at an angle, jutting out. She touched it. She gripped it.

'If you've got that far, you'd better go on, Master Horace. Go on! Let me see you do it!' She insisted as I hesitated. Unable to bring myself to do it in her presence, I leant away from her.

She took hold of my prick again and began rubbing it, muttering, 'Oh, you naughty naughty boy! You shouldn't rub it yourself! You shouldn't!'

Her other arm went round my back and she dropped on to one knee. She was working away, her face flushed. She held my prick, rather daintily between thumb and two first fingers, with her little finger cocked out straight, in the genteel fashion she observed while holding a tea-cup. I already had enough sense to know Mother would never be called. I was still speechless, but now with exaltation. Although I was still in my anti-girl phase, Beatrice was somewhat too old to be exactly classed as a girl, and the pleasure was exquisite.

'Lay on the bed,' she said. As I did so, she closed the door. Then she climbed on with me.

For the first time, I was horizontal with a girl beside me.

We were both trembling. She lay half on top of me, still tossing me off, but now from a rather less advantageous angle. She kissed me at the same time. Without knowing what I was about, I was reaching up under her dress, sliding my hand up over her black cotton stockings, feeling her leg. Suddenly aware of what I was doing, I hesitated.

'Go on!' she said. She pressed my hand right up into her crotch. I slid my hand under the leg of her knickers as she opened her legs—and there for the first time the genuine article lay fluttering in my grasp, damp and furry and indescribably exciting. Gripping it, I held on tightly while she rubbed away. Now a strange sensation overcame me, originating I knew not where, but slowly encompassing my whole body.

I lay back in a swoon, my hand slipping from her fanny, gasping, while she kissed my open mouth and tossed me off like fury. The feeling rose and flowered and burst magnificently, and my body seemed to churn into dozens of delighted particles. It was my first orgasm. Flinging my arms about Beatrice, I lay with my head on her breast; so we remained for a lingering interval.

The beauty of this event left me dazzled for a long while. There was awe in my attitude towards it, awe for my own hidden capacities, awe for the staggering generosity of women who could provoke such wonders, and a little awe left over for a world that allowed such clandestine glories to occur. I saw that England and its fair inhabitants might indeed be worth the contents of an Indian gold-mine.

Part of my wonder resided in the fact that what had happened was an unique event. Nor did I make any particular move to alter this state of affairs.

I had faith that such pleasures, such revelations, would recur. Unfortunately, Beatrice decided otherwise. Although she had been overwhelmed by lust when she saw me standing posturing naked before the mirror, in cooler blood, later, she must have been stricken by conscience to think she had seduced (if that was what she had done) a boy of twelve. She resolved she must not touch me again, and proceeded to evade me about the house.

When I realised this I was mortified. At the time it did not occur to me that she might see anything sinful in what we had done; if she avoided me it could only be because she did not much like me. I lay in wait for her, trying to catch her alone in the kitchen, or on the landing upstairs, once venturing desperately up the second flight of stairs to the servants' quarters, creeping into her little room, pleading with her—only to be turned away.

During this miserable period I masturbated myself for consolation, and Ann also did it to me, but there was no transcendence, although I now had orgasms on every occasion—still without ejaculating. I achieved higher feelings on my own, when I could create fantasies about Beatrice. It never occurred to me to try to excite Ann; seemingly, it never occurred to her that she could be excited.

The summer holidays came, I returned from school with an adverse report. Father said nothing about it; Mother told me he was very angry, and disappointed in me; but he always was being disappointed in me.

[62]

As usually happened, we went to our bungalow by the sea. Father drove us down and came to visit us at the weekends, living alone at home during the week, looked after by one of the maids. The other maid came to the seaside with us. On this occasion I was mournfully glad to find Beatrice was coming with us.

I wish I could remember more of that little darling. The real Beatrice has long since been obnubilated by the long years of my fantasies about her. Nothing comes back to me except the thrilling feel of her fanny between my fingers, elusive and plump. She could not have been more than nineteen. I adore her still!

She was forced to reach our bungalow by train and local bus, a journey involving half a dozen changes, because it would never have done to have had your maid in the car with you, even if you could have crammed her into your little hot black Rover.

Our family holiday tradition was wearing a little thin by this date. The bungalow was now rather cramped for us, although Father had had a large living room tacked on and had divided the old living room into two bedrooms. On this occasion it was raining dismally when we arrived. Nelson, too, was in sober mood. His School Certificate exams were looming over him, and he arrived armed with a parcel of schoolbooks to work at. In my wretchedness I had confided in him about the Beatrice affair; he had promised to speak to Beatrice on my behalf, but nothing had come of it.

That dull day of our arrival comes back to me well! I took my sister's hand and we ran down to the edge of the sea in our macs. She hunted for funny stones, calling in delight. I flung driftwood into the waves. More time passed than we knew, until heavier rain drove us back to the bungalow. Mother had lit the big oil lamps with their bulging white translucent shades, and everything looked homely and welcoming as Ann paraded her treasures on the table. Where was Father? I asked. Since the weather was so unpromising, he had had a cup of tea and started the drive home immediately.

And he had not thought to say goodbye to Ann and me!

As it happened, the weather improved the next day. It became bright and dry, with a little cold hard wind sneaking along the sands, entirely typical of the North Norfolk coast. Ann and I loved the wide beaches, and played on them contentedly all day. Ann could swim like a little dolphin; Nelson was a good diver; but I could swim farther than either of them, and farther underwater.

One morning, Mother decided she would buy herself a dress, and took Ann with her to King's Lynn for the day; Ann liked the train ride.

Beatrice could look after the boys. By now, I was fed up with Beatrice, and ran off to the beach as soon as I had waved goodbye to Mother and Ann. I joined some brown and ragged boys in a game of cricket on the great expanse of sand. They were bigger than I, and tough, and to their chagrin I bowled them all out one by one, until they chased me savagely off the beach.

As I made my way back to the bungalow, some instinct made me go very quietly. I threw my gym shoes into the hedge and crept up the sandy path. Most of the windows were open—I must have caught the odd murmur of voices. Bumble-bees were in all the snapdragons by the front porch.

Gliding round to one of the big side windows, I stealthily raised an eye over the sill, heart beating heavily with presentiments of evil. This window had belonged to the old living room. A partition now divided it unequally in two. The large part lit my mother's bedroom, the smaller, the maid's room.

For reasons of comfort, Nelson and Beatrice had elected to lie on the double bed in my mother's room. They were between bouts. He was naked except for a flannel shirt, and had removed his spectacles. She still wore all her clothes bar her knickers, which had been kicked on to the floor. The rest of her clothes were bundled up round her breasts. He was kissing her stomach. I could not see Beatrice's face.

After a moment, Nelson moved so that I could see he bore a flaming erection. He opened her legs and knelt between them as if he was going to to enter her, but she sat up and cupped his prick in her hands, staring at it deeply as if it were a crystal ball in which she could read her future. I thought, My God, she really likes it! with a sort of terror.

She lay back, and there was a lot of fumbling while he tried to get it in the hole. Unfortunately, I really could not see this part of the business at all. Somehow it wasn't right, or else they were both so amateur. Nelson went off heat slightly and rested beside her. They started rubbing each other and moaning slightly. Now I could see a little glimpse of pink under his fingers. It looked maddening—I must have been half-way through the window by now, my eyes nearly bursting from my head.

Nelson tried again, rolling on to her, and this time, pushing between them, he slid his prick up her, to general groans of delight, and began slyly to move his bum up and down, up and down, his legs straight between her opened and crooked ones.

Intense fevers obscured my senses. I slid away from the window, tumbling to my knees on the ground, falling among the flowers, discovering as I did so that, in my fascination, I had unknowingly dragged my penis from its lair and wanked it furiously, with inevitable results. I was somewhat vexed that it had happened without my being aware of it, and also scared in case anyone had seen me from the road; but there appeared to be nobody about and presently I picked myself up and peeped in the window again.

I saw their enviable climax take place, that thrilling twitching of limbs! Almost at once, Beatrice sat up and grabbed a towel to wipe herself—doubtless fearing the consequences of her love-making. To do this, she perched on the edge of the bed and opened her legs wide. From my position, I would have had a glorious view of all her secrets but, after one quick thirsty glance, I had to slide out of sight, since she would have looked directly at me had she lifted her head.

All I had seen drove me absolutely insane with lust. Little juicy twots seemed to burst open inside my brain! I ran round the bungalow with my prick out, wanking furiously, barefoot, uncaring. Finally I flung myself on a pile of grass-cuttings and shot my bolt again, body heaving.

The misery was by no means over.

Beatrice made us a scratch lunch and we ate it on the balcony in a heavy and intermittent silence.

Afterwards, Nelson came to me with a clenched fist to set under my nose and said, 'If you tell anyone what happened this morning I swear I'll brain you!'

I was overcome with anguish. How did he

know I knew? Later I discovered that he had seen me rolling and wanking on the grass from his bedroom window, and divined what had driven me to that extremity. But I have wondered since whether, in fact, he had not noticed or at least sensed me at his window, and derived a certain amount of additional pleasure from showing off his capabilities to a younger brother.

I looked at him in a beaten way and said, 'Let me do it with Beatrice, Nelson!'

'You're too young. It isn't good for you.' He was kindly now. 'Come on, I'll toss you off, if you like!'

'Don't want you to!' But he was opening my flies and, whatever *I* felt, my little weapon was not adverse to the idea.

'Fetch Beatrice!' I begged.

'Ssh! Get on the bed and I'll give you a really good going.'

'Oh, if you must!'

It was a flimsily constructed bungalow, and the speculative builder who put it up had not intended that it should keep secrets. Beatrice had been suspicious, or at least uneasy; she now appeared in the doorway, clutching a dishcloth.

The shock of seeing us in that incriminating attitude triggered off her 'I'll tell your mother' threats; equally, the sight of a male organ drove her forward.

I ran squealing to her, prick in hand, offering

it as lovers offer bunches of flowers. I begged her to let me do to her what Nelson had done, swearing I was not too young, that I would keep the secret.

Over my head, angrily to Nelson, she said, 'You rotten little bastard, you *told* him!'

'He saw us!' Nelson said.

They stared at each other.

Anxious that they should concentrate on me, anxious to make as many concessions as possible, I said, 'Please, Beatrice, please, at least do me once — I don't mind if you do Nelson at the same time, please!'

'I shall have to tell your father,' she said wretchedly, seeing herself in too deep for anything other than violent extrication.

Nelson turned pale. He put an arm round her and an arm round me. 'Don't be frightened, Beatrice. You know Horace knows all about it— he's growing up! He won't hurt you. He won't tell anyone if you just do it to him quickly, will you, Horace?'

Of course I protested that I would not tell a soul. We both began to work on Beatrice. I managed to get her to clutch my prick, which alone was balm, although my anxieties were such that I had lost my hard; she looked down at it in a puzzled fashion.

Between us, with protestations and persuasions, we managed to get her to sit on the edge of my

[69]

bed. Nelson now unbuttoned; his prick was flying again; he brought it forth as if it were an additional prop to our argument. Possibly we both felt she could not resist the sight of two cocks; possibly we were right. Suddenly she made up her mind. Shrugging us away, she went off quickly and returned with her towel. Then she lay back resignedly on the bed and let us have our way.

When I lifted her skirts I discovered to my joy and surprise that she had not bothered to put on any knickers since her last encounter (I had no idea how easily knickers came off, suspecting they probably buttoned in obscure places, just as pants did in those days). So there was her curly-haired little cunt, smiling meekly up at me between her legs!

It delighted me, and it terrified me. When she opened her legs it did look incredibly large, the unknown made palpable. It also appeared somewhat complicated, lacking the simple classical lines of my own organ. But it felt good and welcoming, and as I touched it, my waning organ revived. I caught, too, just a scent of the quarry, putting me in mind of the smell I had sniffed on my fingers after my first meeting with this forbidden toy. That was all that was needed to add steel to the backbone.

Beatrice looked at me, sober and keen. Without ever having seen that expression before, I knew she was eager.

I was in a terrific hurry to get in. But she guided me, and I felt the lips of her vagina take and suck at my tip, and then I sunk into that devouring passageway. So much can be described in words; but of all the flooding inspirations which filled me it is impossible to speak. Secret compartments opened in my heart.

It vexes me now that I cannot remember more. I believe orgasm came just on that miraculous contact. For, as I rolled off, Nelson was still pulling himself towards ejaculation by the side of the bed.

During that holiday, and while we were still at the seaside, I had my thirteenth birthday, and Father came to a great decision.

I suppose I was a worry to my parents. I still had temper fits, I was not doing well at school, and now I had become very solitary and morose, and would hardly speak to Nelson.

My parents could not guess at the torments that raged in my being. I had imagined that once Beatrice allowed me to screw her, she would allow me to do so every day. Far from it. She and Nelson made it quite clear that that one and only time was my reward for keeping silent. I must expect no more rewards. It was unhealthy.

Jealousy corroded me. Every morning Mother

would take Ann and me down to the beach. Nelson, pleading that he had to study, would be allowed to stay in the bungalow—where Beatrice was supposedly cleaning the house and preparing a picnic lunch to bring down to the sands. I knew what they were doing. Always before my eyes was a vision of them doing it, and the vision of how marvellous Beatrice looked with her clothes up by her armpits.

At the seaside, Ann seemed to have lost all interest in sexuality. She swam and ran and roamed the dunes and built castles, and forgot that she had ever tossed me off. No, once she did it to me as I stood naked among the dunes, flaunting myself; she put both hands round it, working from the front, tongue half-out, as when she was colouring a picture. But I was too mixed up to confide my problems to her.

Nelson hated me, seeing me as a threat to his enjoyment. He would not answer my anxious questions. On one occasion he did drop this hostile attitude when he discovered from Beatrice a piece of news so galvanising, and at first so incredible, that he was forced to share it with me.

According to Beatrice, when we were all at the seaside my father screwed Brenda every day. Brenda was our other maid, an older girl who did not sleep in. How old was she? Ancient to us, but considerably younger than Father—probably in her late thirties.

It was not Brenda who interested us: it was Father. We had never considered him capable of screwing. We had no evidence at all (our own existence was so permanent a thing that we could not include it as evidence) that our parents knew anything about sex. And now, here was Father taking his trousers down and kissing. . . . more than kissing. . . . old Brenda. . . . Amazing! If it was true. . . .

So it was with a great deal of covert interest that I regarded my father when he appeared next weekend. Supposing it was true that he did it. Perhaps Brenda *made* him do it to her! Perhaps she had some secret hold over him! Perhaps she owed the bank an incredible amount of money, and had threatened not to pay unless he shagged her regularly every lunch hour. Or perhaps they did it in the evenings. Before or after high tea. I visualised it as a very formal affair, with neither speaking to the other. Sometimes I pictured them doing it in the bank, on top of the counter, bedding down on lumpy money-bags.

Father appeared much as usual. You could never tell with adults. He came down on to the beach with us, changed into his fierce black-and-red-striped bathing costume, and swam with us, and later drank tea out of our bakelite cups and ate squashy tomato sandwiches that tasted elusively of the greaseproof paper.

In the evening, when the oil lamps were lit, he

took me into my bedroom, saying he wished to speak to me privately.

My heart somersaulted in my breast. Beatrice had told him of my sins! He was going to preach to me.

Or—far worse!—he was going to tell me what he had been up to with Brenda, man to man!

Or worse again. He was going to do both. 'Young man, I know what you've been up to with one maid, so I'm going to tell you what I've been up to with the other. I'm going to tell you in such revolting detail that you will never look at a woman again. For a start, I don't have a cock like your silly little thing. I have a much bigger one, made of flesh and cork, which I screw on. . . .'

It was nothing like that. He had to tell me that he was going to send me away to boarding school next term. It was for my own good.

I found myself crying and saying that he didn't love me and Mummy didn't love me, or they wouldn't send me away. He said that was entirely untrue; they loved me very much, and it was because they loved me very much that they were sending me away, because at boarding school I would learn much more than I did now, and so would be able to be a success in the world in later life.

Being a success in the world in later life sounded to me as repulsive as, and somewhat similar to, climbing out of one's grave and going to be judged on Judgement Day. I pleaded that I would do whatever they wanted, that I would work harder, that I would never have a temper fit again, and so on, if only I might be allowed to stay at home.

Father was much upset. He made me blow my nose and told me not to be a baby. He hated scenes; he hated to see his children sad; but he had already booked a place for me at a large grey public school up in the Peak District, not too far (so *he* said) from home.

It must have been in his mind that neither Nelson nor I were doing very well at school; nor had our grammar school a very high reputation. While it was too late for change in Nelson's case, there was still a chance for me to enjoy a better education. He loved us and wanted us to do well, just as he had done in his modest way.

To me, the matter looked very different. The fact that I was being sent away when my elder brother wasn't, told me enough. With my guilt-laden conscience I decided that they just could not stand me any more. Hadn't Mother always wanted to go away from me? Wasn't this just a clever way of detaching me? On this point I dared not confront her directly, but I made a direct assault on her emotions, weeping and sulking and being sick and having tantrums, and begging her not to let me go.

She was as patient and sweet as could be with

me. But there was nothing she could do to alter the march of events. Daddy had decided it would be good for me to go to Branwells, and to Branwells I must go. I had better be a man about it. Once I got there, I should enjoy it. Besides, there would be lots of boys to play with. . . .

The delights and horrors of English public schools have been thoroughly explored before now. Not that that would deter me from writing an account of my own experiences. But boredom confronts me at the whole prospect. The four years I passed, not too uncomfortably, at rainy, draughty Branwells in stony Derbyshire, were not a period of any real sexual development. Although I was never greatly ill-treated, and never greatly ill-treated anyone, the experience as a whole, in its negativity, had a depressing effect on me. So, except for one cherished episode, the whole period can be passed over in summary.

At first I was utterly crushed by the newness of everything: the newness, the size, and the discomfort of everything. There were three hundred boarders at Branwells, living a prison life without appeal to any code of justice. We were beaten, often violently, by prefects and masters. We formed little gangs among ourselves, we insulted each other, we cheated in class, wanked in the dormitories and fought in the corridors; only on the rugger fields did we play fair, because fairness was one of the rules of the game. Not until we reached the peace and sublimity of the sixth form was it possible to become a little civilised and form something like real friendships. By the time I got to that haven, Neville Chamberlain was flying about calming Adolf Hitler and we were digging useless trenches behind the sanatorium in case of air raids.

At first, I was almost glad of the relief from sex which the hectic school routine provided. This feeling wore off as term progressed. I only gradually became aware that there was a tremendous amount of furtive sexual activity in progress all round me.

Comparing notes later in life with other survivors of the public-school system, I realise that Branwells was a fairly humane institution. Sexual bullying was none. Nobody ever forced me to do anything I did not want to do; although a group of prefects once made me bare myself for inspection, and one of them stirred my little weapon with the end of a cane, they did not abuse me.

Sex activity was limited almost entirely to masturbation or mutual masturbation (known as 'insurance' after the Mutual Insurance Company, who had an office near the school, to the general edification); sodomy and buggery never seemed to enter anyone's head, and would have been frowned on; fellatio was known, but it was regarded as almost as unmanly to be the sucked as the sucker. The code for behaviour in masturbation was also strict, and an interesting sidelight on British middle-class life it affords, for it may be expressed thus: one does not wank one's friends. Possible wankees were drawn in the main from three groups: one's neighbours or near neighbours in the dormitory, however poor or even hostile one's relations with them were during the day; one's neighbours in the form room, however poor or even hostile one's relations with them at other times; and the youngest boys.

Considering that almost everyone wanked someone, the amount of discretion involved in these activities was considerable. One's friends were not to be wanked; they might be used as repositories of wanking confidences; but strict followers of the unwritten code remained silent upon all vital wanking issues—that is, how often one wanked and when and with whom. To be caught in solitary masturbation was a disgrace.

As soon as it was lights-out in the dormitories, an intense but resonant silence fell. It was not considered good form if one allowed one's bedsprings to creak, although there were a few unfortunates with bad beds whose springs always creaked; these boys invariably lost face, or took to exercising their rampant genitals at other times of the day. There was none of that free-and-easy camaraderie that exists in certain barrack rooms in the Army, where the lance-corporal, as he switches off the lights, yells jovially, 'Pricks—Atten-shun! Take up wanking positions! On your marks, ready, steady—go! Them as can't wank go through the motions.'

To the meretricious Branwells' rule of absolute secrecy in the midst of absolute activity there were occasional exceptions, when more than two or three boys were simultaneously involved, or when everyone went on a sex-jag.

The most communal of such occasions was the Maginot Line. This took place in the dormitories, usually as a celebration after the school had won a sporting event. It consisted of a line of chaps, forming up between the beds, catching hold of the prick of the man on his right, and rubbing when a signal was given. Sometimes, an element of competition was added by seeing who could make whom come first.

A ritual which had more of the element of a trial in it was the solitary pilgrimage, when one member of the dormitory (which might hold up to forty boys) would decide to go round to each bed in turn, administering a tossing-off at each.

This was a rather pleasant ritual. The production-line effect of the proceedings relieved them of any embarrassment they might have for the shyer members of the dormitory. A pilgrimage also permitted the more horrid boys (those considered too obnoxious to be wanked by others) to get their share of the general sexual charge, since it was a point of honour on good pilgrimages to include everyone; no refusals were expected or allowed. The pilgrim finished his sacred round with a painfully stiff penis. He was then allowed to give himself relief, or to choose anyone he liked to do it for him.

'Insurance' clubs also flourished. In my second term I was voted into such a club in our corner of the dormitory. My bed was the penultimate along one end of a line of beds; the chap in the end bed, I, and the next two along, formed a club of four. We took it in turn each night to creep out of bed and toss off each of the others; we could do ourselves simultaneously, or let the others help, but the rota had to be filled each night. Neither wanker nor wanked was allowed to back out of his duty under any pretext, unless he was playing in a house or school game next day, in which case he was allowed to conserve his strength.

We founded this club on the second night of term. It lasted for almost six weeks, until half-term, when a flu epidemic gave us an excuse to forget it. It was enjoyable enough; four fine able weapons were involved; the one snag was that it took so long to make Partington come that we got bored at his bed. The rest of us were comfortably quick about it. Rivers needed only a few strokes to send him off, especially at first.

This club was good for me, because I was somewhat shy of the whole business at first, but our form of 'insurance' permitted the relationships to be totally impersonal. No affection was involved.

It also allowed me to reopen my investigation of uncircumcised penises, since it happened that the other three members of the club were all endowed with what I had not. That extra piece seemed to me an extraordinary luxury. It drew back so sumptuously, and was juicy underneath, not unlike Beatrice's fanny. Smith's foreskin peeled back on its own accord, as his penis swelled to erection. Partington had inches of it, and could only draw it back with difficulty; he liked to be manipulated with his foreskin up, whereas Rivers preferred it with his drawn right back. This variety fascinated and troubled me.

One reason why it troubled me sounds laughable now, although it was far from laughable at the time.

Although I said that Ann was uninterested in sex while we were holidaying at the seaside, this was not entirely the case. She had been keeping alert. When Father changed on the beach to come swimming with us, Ann watched very carefully while pretending to be playing with the sand, and discovered—or told us she had discovered—that the end of his penis was covered with skin.

So why, I asked myself, had he taken Nelson's and my foreskins away? It seemed an unfriendly thing to do. I worried about it, and much of my masturbation at this time was directed towards massaging the skin in the hope it might grow back again.

Most of the sexual activity at Branwells took place after dark. But it survived vigorously during the day, behind playing-field hedges, behind buildings, in changing rooms, in baths, in class, in the laboratories, in the school chapel, in corners, in the library.

Harper Junior was particularly fond of the library for his form of exhibitionism. He certainly had something to exhibit; it would have been a pity to have wasted it on the hours of darkness.

The younger Harper brother was in many respects a complete nonentity. His eyes swam behind pebble glasses, he suffered from a painful series of boils, he was flat-footed. He was no good at games, no good in class. The only thing that redeemed him—and that splendidly in our eyes—was his mighty weapon.

The male organ comes in two kinds. There is the sort such as I possess which is tiny when in a state of quiet but expands enormously when erect; and there is the kind that looks very large when limp but does not expand greatly when erect. Of whichever kind, almost all penises are between six and eight inches long when on the alert. Harper Junior's prick was eleven inches long when limp and a foot long when erect. Or it could have been a foot long when limp and thirteen inches erect. I know a foot came into it somewhere. And this was before he reached puberty and acquired what were always termed 'ball-hairs' at Branwells.

Harper Junior's prick was famous throughout the school. Chaps came from other houses and other forms to view it. They never tired of looking. Harper Junior never tired of flashing it, day and night. Day and night he was besieged by people begging him to let them have a wank at that fine cylindrical object.

My turn came behind a padded leather armchair in the library. It rose before me in all its glory, the foreskin not quite long enough, so that a glimpse of the knob was temptingly revealed. I began to move the flesh almost reverently up and down. Harper Junior watched it and me craftily.

'Do you want to suck it?' he asked.

'No. Why?'

'Lots of them like to suck it. *I* can suck it. Look!'

He bent forward, opening his mouth, and took the end in easily, sucking with great relish.

'You can finish me off,' he said generously, in a minute.

I did.

Sister caught Harper Junior naked in the dormitory once, flapping his prick against his stomach.

'Put that thing away at once, Harper!' she said, and passed on unperturbed.

She was the only female allowed in the dormitories, a small hard plump military figure that even the most randy senior boy could never hope or wish to seduce. Sometimes she marched through the changing rooms where dozens of boys were stark naked and nobody paid any more attention than if it had been the gym instructor, an old army sergeant.

Some might say that more attention should have been paid to the gym instructor. But I never recall any cases of boys being seduced by masters or staff—had it happened, the news would have spread round the school at once. Mutual masturbation was rife, but homosexuality was virtually non-existent; perhaps the elaborate codes guarded against it. Certainly the codes, with their embargo on emotion, helped to damp down affectionate attachments that might lead to later disturbances; on the other hand, they tended to promote cold-

ness of temperament and concentration on the
organ, as they did in my case. For all that, within
the insane context of a public school, I believe
they acted to protect the maximum number. Of
course, they could not protect the oddity like
Harper Junior. I'm sure he came to a bad end—
a bad but, from his point of view, probably enjoyable end.

The negative aspects of public-school life
extended their influence into the holidays. Holidays were brief in comparison with term-time and
this formed a barrier to making friends for anyone
who tended to be shy, as I increasingly found
myself to be. Relationships with old girl friends
like Hilda and Sheila were difficult to establish.
The casual ways of childhood had been lost.

One holiday, in desperation, I approached
Margaret Randall, the kindergarten stripper,
who now wore high heels and worked in the
branch of F. W. Woolworth's just opened in town.
I took her to the cinema to see a sloppy film of
her choosing, and held her hand in the darkness.
Afterwards, when I tried to kiss her, she told me
to clear off. I never had the nerve to remind her
I had once seen her flashing her pretty little cunt
on top of the school-room table; probably I
should have done; it might have worked wonders.

Some interfering idiot saw me with Margaret
and reported it to my mother. She was very sweet

and gentle with me, while making it clear to me that in 'our position' I must not be seen out with a girl who worked in Woolworth's. She did not really like my going into Woolworth's at all. It was a cheap place. And besides—well, I was a bit young for girl friends, wasn't I? Why didn't I try and be better company for Ann?

Okay, if she wanted it that way. I let my sister toss me off again, although by now I felt this was slightly childish. One morning I made her do it three times straight off, which greatly impressed her. With Nelson I was more contained. He was very withdrawn now, studying for an endless succession of exams that lay between him and his chance of being an architect. He was courting a very dull girl called Caroline Cathcart, whom I thought as stupid as her name. Happily, she did not last too long. Nelson and I entered into no confidences about her sexual proclivities. Naively, I wondered if Nelson had forgotten about sex; something in the forbidding aspect of Caroline Cathcart encouraged this illusion.

'Are you still bashing your bishop?' I asked him once, but he told me not to be cheeky. As for the maids, Beatrice was engaged to be married, and Brenda had left. According to Ann's report, Brenda left without any rows or dramatic disclosures, so we never knew whether Father had been lucky there.

Dramatic disclosures were something of which

we stood in great need. All unknown to us, our
thirsty souls needed art and revelation. In this
respect, public-school life, with its constant minor
crises, was to be preferred to the dull security of
home.

'Your father's trying to listen to the docu-
mentary,' Mother would say reprovingly in the
evening, as Ann and I grew noisy over a game of
cards. All Father's art and revelation came
through the B.B.C. He did like a good docu-
mentary. While he was being educated we were
being repressed—by his pained looks and Mother's
indignant 'Ssssh's!'. We hated documentaries,
and the News, and the Fat Stock Prices—to which
Father, when at home, would listen absorbedly.

Ann's hate and mine were uninhibited. Nelson,
as elder son, veered between taking our side and
taking Father's. He could occasionally be tempted
on to our side, and we would all three burst into
helpless giggles. Sometimes he would stalk out in
pretended anger, and sneak round to the pub for
a half-pint of bitter.

Apart from the B.B.C., there was nothing.
Nothing except the cinema. We visited it whenever we could, under Nelson's charge. There was
our art and our revelation; it never entered our
heads that it might be bad art and false revelation.
Everything that those giant slow-moving grey
figures of myth did was amazing. Under their
spell we learnt how the big world turned, how the

wicked never prospered, and how women had to
have flowers and moonlight before they would
let you get near them. But from them too we first
learnt to listen to the marvellous unafraid noise
of jazz and relish the extraordinary faces and
sounds of black musicians. We never had enough
of the cinema, because we were never allowed too
much of it.

At that period, and for long after, I was desperately grateful to Hollywood for opening up life
and art to me. Now I'm less sure. They got the
perspectives all wrong. The world depended on
them, and they flogged it a lot of sentimental
middle-class humbug!

The one bit of broadcasting we all enjoyed as a
family was 'Music Hall', which came on every
Saturday night. Mother used to bake a big coco-
nut cake, which we settled down to guzzle as the
band struck up 'Back to Those Happy Days'. The
comics were my favourites, particularly the filthy
ones like Max Miller, though it was agony to
sit there bursting with laughter while outwardly
looking stupid, as if you didn't see the jokes. If it
became too bad you could always pretend you
had choked on a crumb of cake.

As I grew up, the girl problem grew, if anything,
more acute. The pride and delight we experienced

at school when we first managed to generate semen proved something of an illusion in the big world. If there was one thing girls dreaded it was semen. Semen was the devil. By natural association of ideas, this dread seemed to spread to pricks. What a girl can innocently enjoy at ten, she stands in horror of at fifteen. Or such was my experience in our snobbery-bound little bourgeois circles in the thirties. The Pill has changed matters nowadays.

All the girls I was officially permitted to mix with had been scared by nonsense tales. They and the boys were fobbed off with bunkum about not touching anyone you weren't engaged to. The language of warning was vague, and perhaps the more powerful for that. Also, with the pernicious influence of the cinema, everything was supposed to be done 'romantically', which meant talking and courting and taking ages over it and hanging about for full moons and so on.

Later in my teens I suffered depths of social and moral agony trying to fuck girls. They wanted it, they knew I wanted it, but everything was against us. For a start, they had been taught to say 'Oh, please don't do that!' and 'Oh, no, Horry, you mustn't!' and so on—phrases which brought some fellows on well, but only damped my enthusiasm.

Then there was trouble about where you went to do it. Boys and girls alike, we had no money in those days, only a feeble bit of pocket-money carefully designed to keep you a kid as long as possible. You couldn't buy a hotel room or anything—and probably would not have dared to if you had had the money, because the hotel owners would instinctively have been against you, against life, against fun, against pricks, against cunts. England was a filthy little hole to grow up in in the thirties—bitterly impoverished for the poor, bitterly repressive for the middle classes.

Repression: it is part of civilisation, very necessary in society, particularly middle-class society which, my scanty historical knowledge instructs me, only levered its way up into money and respectability by postponing for the first years of its maturity such pleasures as sex. This is one of the attractions of war—the repressions can be shed.

Those horrid middle-class repressions operated strongly in the Stubbs family. The younger Stubbs boy felt them badly in his teens, the time when sexuality is highest. At Branwells there were many boys, like me, who masturbated two or three times every day and gave themselves a treat on Sunday. Digby claimed to do himself every Saturday night until his semen dried up—six or seven wanks one after the other.

And many of the boys were worried to distraction about what they were doing to themselves. They had got the word, often from their fathers, that masturbation would ruin their physiques or send them mad. The warning did not stop them. It often made them do it more, since the subject was more on their minds. Sometimes it forced them into peculiar habits. Beasley wanked himself almost to the point of climax every day and then stopped; only on Saturday night did he allow himself proper satisfaction. Spaldine, who tried to run away from Branwells his first term there, used to press a finger against the base of his penis so as to have orgasm without wasting semen.

In that respect I was lucky; nobody ever represented the pastime to me as anything but enjoyable. I lay back and enjoyed it. But ever since the happy day when Beatrice caught me naked before the mirror I knew there were better things.

The better things, as I say, were hard to come by from girls of my own age and class. They had had a dose of middle-class morality even more severe than the boys.

There was, over everything else, the problem of babies. If, by some miracle of perseverance and guile, you managed to dip your wick, the girl would be screaming all the while that she might have a baby. Working-class girls were much better in that respect. *Their* drawback was that they always seemed to have in the background big tough boy friends who would jump out with big tough buddies and attempt to bash you.

The baby problem could be overcome, at least in theory, by using French letters. But French letters had to be bought. It was not just the cash. It was stepping into the little barber's at the end of Chapel Road and actually asking for a packet for a friend. The only time I dared to go in was one day when I thought I was on a sure thing for the evening, a rather plump girl called, so help her, Esmeralda, who belonged to the tennis club I did. I spent about an hour of indecision, riding past the barber's shop and round the corner on my bike, at various speeds. Finally I did go in and buy a packet of three Frenchies.

Esmeralda's parents were common but rich. Nobody had a good word to say for them behind their backs; everyone toadied to them to their faces. I did not like Dad greatly, but Mum was a fat and loving lady, who could call me Horatio as if she took the name seriously; she was rather grand, in her way. They had a big ramshackle house, and Esmeralda and her mum both played the piano and sang—rather well, I thought. They performed all the jolly and rather bawdy music-hall songs, like 'Then Her Mama Went Out, De-Da-De-Da-De-Da-De-Dee' and 'Who Were You With Last Night?' and 'Hello, Hello, Who's Your Lady Friend?'

I was pleased with all that sort of liberal-minded stuff. But on this particular night there wasn't going to be any singing, or anything but screwing, because Esmeralda's mum and dad were going to be in Nottingham and Esmeralda had given me the green light.

She was a cuddly, happy-go-lucky little thing, Esmeralda. I envied her her temperament. She enjoyed a bit of kissing on the sofa, liked it when I tickled her feet and felt and admired her legs.

I slid my hand up farther and whispered, 'Let me have a look up there, love!'

'You can have a look. That won't hurt either of us. But I may as well tell you now, *love*, that you aren't going to get anything more than a look.'

'The sight of it may drive me mad!'

'That's up to you, not me!'

I patted my pocket. 'You don't have to be frightened. I've brought some things.'

The announcement did frighten her. She saw I meant business. The trouble was, I was also frightened, and didn't know whether or not I meant business. I had never worn a French letter.

So I dropped that line of approach and got her friendly again. Bless her, she did let me have a look, a good look, and I dipped my fingers in it and rubbed her, although I had no idea about whether I was tickling the right thing. She didn't even ask for the light off, for which I was grateful. It was marvellously liberating to be able to *see*.

But I could feel my hard-on going soft. I extracted it from my flies and started fumbling with the French-letter packet. I got one out, pushing the other two back into my pocket. I balanced it on my glans penis and began awkwardly to try to roll it down. Esmeralda had been lying back in a languorous posture. She sat up and watched with interest.

I got the damned thing on, wrinkled and repulsive. My hard deflated further. I began rubbing it to keep its spirits up, furious and yet also half-amused at the sight.

She laughed rather contemptuously, and put her hand on it. I let her take over, gaining courage, thinking she was more experienced than I had expected. In a moment I was ready to slide it in. Esmeralda leant back, and was all honey, and her plump thighs wonderfully moist. We were both nervous. It would not go in.

I did not actually know where to put my penis in that chubby pink pocket. I didn't know enough about female anatomy. I had never explored my sister. I pushed and sweated, and the damned French letter meant I could not feel her pleasant parts.

'You're hurting me, love. I'm a virgin—I think you'd better give over!'

Did she invoke that middle-class spectre of virginity to save my face? I don't know. But I was glad enough to desist, and pulled the French letter off in exasperation.

My prick hung limp and ludicrous. Something seemed to expand within me until I believed I was about to choke, remembering that I was soon due to go back to bloody Branwells. With a tremendous effort, blushing red, I managed to say, 'Toss me off, Esmeralda, please!'

Whether or not she had heard the words before, she understood what I meant.

'Come and snuggle by me,' she said. She put my hand on her fanny and grasped my weapon, which immediately showed fight. I kissed her both passionately and lovingly. She was a fine girl. I would have died had I had to return to school without shedding my load in her darling presence, however it was done.

Into the brickwork at the back of the squash courts at Branwells was carved a legend. The lettering read merely 'A. K. DANCER', and underneath the letters was a boldly stylised outline of prick and balls. Behind that rather flashy and mysterious name, Dancer, lay a story known to every one of the three hundred boys at Branwells, its repetition guaranteed by the unknown memorialist.

Dancer had been expelled about ten years before—some years before even the oldest boy had arrived snivelling for his first term. But the name and memory and the legend of Dancer stayed green. For Dancer was the boy who had been caught fucking the matron. He was beaten and expelled. The matron had left too. Dancer had married her, and they lived happily ever after, with several kids.

Has any public school ever had a better or more telling myth?

If Dancer had not existed it would have been necessary to invent him. He represented the secret hopes of all of us that we would somehow escape the awfulness of school to a natural life. Not un-scathed, of course (that was the symbolism of the beating), for every public-school boy very soon becomes a realist. And the expulsion was also a meaningful ingredient. Dancer was sacked; he could never revisit Branwells. We knew that those old boys who came back after they had left school, to lecture and boast of worldly success, were really bores and flops, and probably crypto-homosexuals too, sniffing again the scents of old prowess. We knew that school was a prison. Only suckers returned.

We had one of those plodding school songs, built about the school motto, 'Study and Stand Fast'. A wit had written in an extra verse dedi-cated to Dancer's exploit:

'In Derbyshire's dull dorms,
 On beds and desks and forms,
 When lesser souls abused themselves, outclassed,
 Our Dancer, saint and patron,
 He upped and tupped the matron—

He shafted and came fast!
He shafted and came fu-u-uck-ing fast!'

It chanced that to me fell the opportunity to become a second Dancer.

The short and sergeant-majorly old school sister retired. In her place came a woman of a very different kind, Sister Virginia Traven. 'When she arrived, they called her Virgin for short but not for long,' ran the immediate school joke, for, in that castle of acute female-shortage, it was recognised that she was not exactly incredibly old or incredibly ugly.

Sister Traven was slightly built. She had indeterminate-coloured eyes, which did not always manage to look at you. Her hair was short and tawny, she carried her head rather attractively on one side, as if half in sly jest about life. The old sister had never been in jest about anything.

A mystery surrounded Sister Traven, how the headmaster passed her as safe for a boys' school being the first one. Not that she was less than thirty-five years old, which is a staid old age to schoolboys. She spoke in a rather sibilant and allusive way. And she never came out on to the rugger pitch to cheer the first fifteen; the old sister had never missed a game.

The sister arrived at school at the beginning of what proved to be my last year at Branwells, just when I had secured the position of hooker in the first fifteen. She attracted me from the start, perhaps because it so happened that she was returning to school from a shopping expedition by the same train on which I was reluctantly arriving, and she invited me to ride the two miles from the station to school with her in the school car (I had carried her bag to the car). If I was struck dumb on that ride, it was chiefly because she was registering on me.

I wanted to register on her. Playing in the first fifteen was the ideal way to do it—until I found that she never bothered to watch the game. This made her very unpopular with most of the school. We had a vote on it in the sixth, to which I had now ascended, and it was carried by a narrow margin that, since her gesture was more insulting to the headmaster than to the boys, she was okay. Nobody was rat enough to suggest that she might not be interested in rugger.

During a vote taken only a week later it was decided that she was already being screwed by the music master. Nobody was rat enough to suggest that she might not be interested in sex. ('But dear old Chopin is as queer as a coot, darling—I'd have thought you boys were sharp enough to see *that*!'—thus Virginia, when I put it to her a few months later.)

Slowly we pieced together a bit of news here and a rumour there. Sister was arty. Sister had actually been seen sketching, all wrapped up and sketching bloody fucking Six Sisters. Six Sisters was a hated local landmark, six—actually five by that time—miserable stunted trees to which we had to run once a fortnight, exposed to all the inhospitable gales of Derbyshire. And Sister wanted to paint them! Her stock fell even lower in the junior school. I joined the art club.

I was one of the school slobs, rough but not aggressive (despite occasional bouts of old enemy temper), plodding rather than clever, jocose rather than witty. My friends and I formed the sporty and philistine side of the sixth, still reading Frank Richards' stories about Greyfriars and St. Jims—because, we said defensively, we were amused that the smoking and drinking (and, by inference, the pulling off, for who could imagine Tom Merry with a hard-on?) which went on at those colleges was always done by slackers, whereas at Branwells most of the venery was committed by the stars of the first fifteen. We were on good terms with the arty half of the form, even though they read Conrad and that ass R. L. Stevenson. But it was felt by everyone, including myself, that I was an incongruous figure in the art club.

Despite the incongruity, I did rather well. I discovered I could paint. During my second term in the art club I was out painting the Six Sisters myself, when not playing rugger. By then I was big enough to belt anyone who laughed.

In other ways my horizons were widening. I became interested in socialism, and that in a curious way.

Most of my sexual liaisons were with fellows of about my own age. But a much younger boy called Brown had caught my attention. Brown was in my dormitory, and had distinguished himself by being the youngest boy ever to make a pilgrimage round the beds—generally, the younger members were more sinned against than sinning. Brown, however, was keen. Keen on everything and sex most of all. He had bright ideas, with a natural flair for the erotic; after I had spent a couple of hours in bed with him I felt he was destined to go far—and downwards all the way.

He confessed to me that he was in love with another boy in the sixth. Torturing him by threatening to leave him on the brink of orgasm, I got from him that this boy was Webster. I burst out laughing, because Webster was someone whom none of us took seriously. He spoke with an affected 'upper-class' drawl—I believe it was affected, although he never entirely dropped it; he could increase it in class, in order to infuriate masters. His parents were known to be well heeled—his father was someone high up in Imperial Tobacco. But Webster was a socialist, or a communist, for neither he nor we were too sure of the difference; he had a catch-phrase, and used to preach to us that things would be different after 'the absolutely bloody revolution'. It was hard to visualise him as Brown's 'lover' (a word, incidentally, that transgressed the Branwells code).

Through our mutual interest in Brown we got together for an 'insurance', the three of us. This was behind an outbuilding at Rowe's Farm, a couple of miles from school. With rubber bands, we coupled our pricks together, Webster's and my turgid black things on the outside, Brown's elegant pink-and-white weapon in the middle, like a grotesque sandwich of cod's roe between two salamis. Webster's tool had been badly scarred by the rite of circumcision, and we were all scarred temporarily by the rubber bands before we were finished. On the way back to school, Webster chatted about all the injustices in England, how wrong it was to have servants, and so on.

'One glorious day, laddies, the down-trodden workers of Britain will arise and free themselves, and the skivvies of England will dashed well knife their masters in their beds.'

'Will the skivvies jump into the beds of the young masters?' Brown asked.

'Yes, and cut off their little rigid plonks!'

What fascinated me even more than that particular vision was the fact that Webster actually knew working men, and showed no particular antipathy for them, although, with his accent, he would surely have been one of the first to go under when they rose on the day of absolutely bloody revolution. His outlook was novel in my experience. I knew only the distaste and fear with which my mother and father and their friends regarded the workers. Even Liberals were bad enough, but the workers. . . . Father hated to see them drawing the dole, believing that the principle of giving money away was wrong. He had been heard to call the destitute of the town, ironically, 'our non-banking friends'.

'Non-washing, you mean,' Mother said. It was not their financial so much as their hygienic habits she loathed.

Now here was Webster saying that these blighters might get the upper hand some time. My parents would be the first to go.

I thought over what Webster said for a long while before asking him, some days after the rubber-band experiment, 'Supposing the workers do revolt, surely the upper classes won't let them kill off all the middle class?'

He chuckled, richly and patronisingly. 'Stubbs, old man, the upper classes and the aristocracy absolutely hate the bloody guts of the middle classes!'

Art. Sex. Socialism. And the greatest of these was sex. But even sex was changing now. England had recently enjoyed (or suffered) the spectacle of their king relinquishing the throne to marry the woman he loved. For many, the issues arising from this crisis in the monarchy were complex; at Branwells it signified only one thing: that the adult world outside our stony walls was as mad about sex as we were, whatever it hypocritically pretended. And our discussions centred round whether or not Mrs. Simpson was attractive.

The abdication also focussed the attention of the older boys more sharply on women. Whatever we did with other boys, *faute de mieux*, it was women we thought about, women we talked about, given a few exceptional boys. Women, we could see, were what we needed, as surely as we lacked them.

Although my father remained aloof from me, never interesting himself in what I did or said, I had by now seen enough penises—'a clutch of penises' was the agreed collective noun—to persuade me that my circumcision, however barbaric, had not been directed at me. It was something bank managers had done to their sons at birth, a sort of caste mark; while the postman's son, a Branwells day-boy, was allowed to keep a foreskin like the end of a fire-hose.

With the allaying of this anxiety, and such minor and common anxieties as to whether my organ functioned as well as, or was as large as, other people's, I began to lose interest in pricks, although not in masturbating; that remained a never-ending pleasure. But the fantasies connected with masturbating became increasingly preoccupied less with Beatrice and more with

Sister Traven, as gradually I managed to win what seemed like her friendship.

In my fantasies Sister sometimes changed shape and became Esmeralda. I had written to Esmeralda and she wrote back, somewhat to my surprise. Her letters were never very long, but they gave me a delight out of all proportion to their length or content. I was none too sure that I did not love Esmeralda.

Did I also love Sister Traven? It must have been some such kind of madness that made me hope to make love to her; or perhaps that is an egocentric view, because many boys at Branwells also dreamed of her in their hard little beds. Not only was she fairly attractive; she was safely inaccessible; and, supposing she were attained, then she was safely old enough to play her role in a motherly way.

She definitely took notice of me individually, I told myself. It needs terrific effort to make yourself individual to an outsider when you are just one of a herd of boys. Overcoming my shyness, or, rather, battling with it all the way, I trotted some of my water-colour sketches along to show her. She actually recognised where one or two of them were supposed to be.

'Do you paint in the holidays?' she asked.

'Oh yes, pretty often.' I had never touched a paintbrush since I was about six.

She asked me where I lived. I told her. She was

pleased. Pleasure always caused her to raise her
eyebrows slightly, as if her pleasure somewhat
amazed her.

'I don't live too far from you. Have you heard
of Traven House? Perhaps you'd like to come
sketching with me some time? I could get the
chauffeur to come and pick you up in the car. We
have some lovely views in our grounds.'

Confusedly, I said it would be lovely. She asked
me what my father did. I said he was a bank
manager, adding defensively, 'And he belongs to
the Rotary Club.'

She told me her father was a rear-admiral. But
he had been retired from the Navy at an early
age because of some disgrace in the China seas.
Now he was a press magnate. Not that I knew
what that was.

Learning to distinguish between facts and fantasies is one of the most vital arts that separates childhood from adulthood. Some people—politicians,
actors, the mentally sick—never acquire the art.

Crisis-time for breaking from the childhood
world where fact and fantasy intermingle comes
in adolescence. In the next school holiday I was
tortured by this crisis.

Sister had promised she would come and take
me out to sketch with her. But was she just playing

a game? Something in her demeanour, that half-jesting expression of hers, suggested that she was.

On the other hand, I had a strong faith in the unlikely. The stately home, the chauffeur, and no doubt the Rolls-Royce, were much more probable and acceptable to me than the whole formidably unlikely organisation of Branwells, which, possibly because I had been sent there at a relatively late age, I could never take for granted.

The one bit of unlikeliness with which I could not come to terms was that this sophisticated woman could love me, or be at all interested in me.

That proved to be fact and not fantasy. She did duly arrive to take me out, although the episode developed in a way I had not expected. My parents did not refuse to let me go out with Sister at the last moment, as I had dreaded they would. Ever since Nelson said jokingly, 'So you've started chasing older women, eh?', I feared my father would read my amorous intentions in my expression and stop everything.

He did not. Nor did Beatrice get Sister on one side and tell her 'what he is really like'. Nor, for that matter, did Sister turn up in a Rolls-Royce. Nor did the Rear-Admiral accompany her!

My relations with Mother were still painful. Although she had by now abandoned the device of threatening to leave us if we were bad, she had developed another tiresome device. If we did anything that pained her, she would cover her eyes and pretend to cry, often actually did cry, and shriek that she was the most miserable of women.

We saw through this at once. Her little darling Ann saw through it first—it was, after all, something of a feminine ploy. Without being taken in, we would nevertheless go boredly to comfort her, since that was the easiest way to silence her and have the embarrassing behaviour out of the way. I believe we held precisely this condescending attitude to her ever since Ann was seven. As this meant that we dropped whatever we were doing that offended her, she thus got her way, and so the situation was self-perpetuating.

That was only a minor tyranny. On the subject of girls, Mother was more difficult. I used to look hungrily at them in the street, the half-challenging, half-inviting stare of the shy man. If they returned the stare, Mother would say, 'Huh, she must be a cheap little bit, giving anyone the glad-eye on the street like that! You want to look out for that kind, my boy—they'll only get you into a lot of trouble!'

When the enemy threatened to materialise into the shape of Sister, she was nonplussed. For this wasn't an ordinary girl friend. This was a member of the staff of Horatio's school, a school official. It was unthinkable that she could—or that he could—well, it was unthinkable. But she had considerable qualms about the outing, and the more I artlessly stressed the painting line, the more

Mother seemed to worry. Father was just sarcastic.

'She's a bit old for you to be going out with, isn't she?'

So she bloody well was. But it just happened that she happened to show a bit of personal interest.

Sister changed the arrangements once or twice, each time to my alarm. But the date held up, though I imagined her saying to the old Admiral over a cocktail, 'It's an absolute bore, Daddy, but I must take the spotty little blighter out, since I promised to do so in a weak moment. *Noblesse oblige* and all that!'

She dropped me a note to say when she would be round to the house to pick me up. Panic! I was the first to panic! Supposing that my mother guessed how much I fancied Sister when she saw us together! Or—supposing Mother and her affectations put Sister off! Supposing the house put her off! Supposing the smell of beer in the living room put her off!

In my anxiety and general uncertainty I failed to let Mother know when Sister was calling for me until a couple of hours before she arrived— and then Mother was also thrown into panic.

'I'll have to change my frock! We'd better have lunch early. Ann and Rosemary will have to play in the back garden. You might have *warned* me, darling! And you say she's one of the Travens of Traven House? What posh circles you move in, Horatio! I've passed Traven House going north—

you can just see it between the trees. She's going
to take you there?'

'Yes, so she said.'

'Lovely! You'd better wear your best suit. I
wish you'd had your hair cut! You will speak up
if the Admiral talks to you, won't you? I'll give
you ten bob, darling, just in case you need it.
We'll have to have her in here—I hope she
doesn't get the whiff of beer or she'll think your
mother's a secret drinker!'

We were still running about in circles, and Ann
had no shoes on, when Sister arrived; she was her
usual quiet self, with that gentle smile which
invited you to be friendly—a 'distinguished'
smile, Ann called it, for even she was impressed.

'But she was so *nice*!' Mother said several times
afterwards, astonished that it should be so. 'Do
you think she'd like to come to tea one day?'

It was cheering to know that Mother and Ann
admired her (though what would they say if
they guessed how I felt?). And it was cheering
that Sister appeared not to notice the aroma of
beer as she stood for a moment, small and individual, in our drawing-room before we left.

The car proved to be, not a Rolls-Royce, not even
a flashy little two-seater, but a battered old Ford.
Sister said something about the other cars not being
available. And we weren't going back to Traven
House. She felt like a drive to Grantham instead.

None of that worried me in the slightest; I

hardly heard what she said. The great triumph
was to be with her, and in the holidays at that!
I sat beside her blushing scarlet from head to
navel: for I saw that she had not bothered to
bring along any paints at all. On the back seat of
the car were not sketching pads but cushions.
Clear evidence she was going to drive me somewhere and seduce me!

There I sat, feverishly clutching my own
sketching block and paints, and now and again
feeling the one French letter in my pocket—the
remaining one of the two left over from the
Esmeralda affair; I had used the other for tossing
off into, and lent it out at school for the same
purpose. Now the unused one was to be put to a
real test, and I was scared at the prospect.

To my relief and disappointment, Sister
intended no seduction. We ate lunch together and
strolled round gazing at the shops. We passed an
Army Recruiting Centre; she put her arm through
mine and asked, 'Which service will you join if
there's a war against Germany?'

We went to the cinema. I held her hand and
nestled against her. And she responded! That
night, safely home again, I bagged an old exercise
book from Nelson and started what I boldly
headed 'A Virginia Journal'. It is before me now,
my first essay in love, and two pages of immature
handwriting are devoted just to the period in the
pictures, when I had the joy of holding her hand.

After the cinema we went for tea to a little teahouse that I uneasily felt did not befit an admiral's daughter. There was nothing flashy about it at all. But she was entirely at ease, so sweet, so smiling, so easy to talk to. She poured my tea for me. I passed the cakes to her. Our table was in one corner, and there were three steps up from the rest of the café to the small room in which we sat.

She told me tantalisingly little about herself; and it was a condition of my life that I could not ask, for fear of seeming rude (had I not always been told 'It's rude to ask questions'?).

She had a big sister whom she adored. I forget her name now, but I know she could ride like the wind.

What's more, she—and Sister—rode in Africa. They had a great gaunt black Zulu as servant for the two sisters. His tongue had been cut out in childhood, and he always carried a spear, but the girls adored him. Their father loved Africa best of all the continents.

She said why didn't I call her Virginia in the holidays? She hoped we could meet again. I grasped the opportunity and asked her if we could meet again the next week. Well, she was going to have to go to London for a few days, but she'd drop me a note.

I thought it was the brush-off. She clutched my hand under the table, drew it on to her knee, smiled lovingly at me, said that she really would write. 'Don't you believe I will?'

'I do believe you will.'

'Honestly I will, love. But I have to go up to London to appear in court—one of my best friends is involved in a divorce case, and I'm a star witness.'

'You lead such an exciting life, Virginia!'

'Divorce is not exciting—it's just cruel. What's the most exciting thing you've ever done, Horatio?'

I told her about the time Nelson and I had been chased by hornets at Hunstanton, and how we had jumped into the sea with all our clothes on to escape from them. Virginia and I both laughed greatly. She was wonderful company.

When she drove me back to our front door, again the agony of crisis. I stared at her. She kissed me fleetingly, just brushing her lips against mine. 'See you soon!'

They asked to look at my sketches as I hurried up to my bedroom.

'I left 'em at Traven Castle,' I said.

My last term at Branwells, although I did not know it then: Summer term, 1939. I thought I had another year to go and Higher School Cert before me. It was the only term I went back eagerly. I knew I was going to see Virginia.

Our second meeting had miraculously come

off. She had been as good as her darling word. We had done much as the first time, and had even managed a brief sort of half-cuddle and a long kiss before parting. Virginia had kissed me! Virginia Traven had kissed me!

At Branwells she seemed only a little more distant, but I realised that if we were going to be lovers, then both sides must exercise caution.

I was made prefect at the beginning of term. This gave me extra freedom. It meant that one could walk about the school on one's own without being questioned, an unheard-of luxury. It also meant that one had a study of one's own in what was called Prosser's Row—a privilege that gave one many sexual advantages, although it is fair to say that few of the prefects took advantage of this, or not very often. We agreed that we were much more civilised than the louts who had been prefects when we arrived as new boys, so long, long before.

Frank Richards was now put behind me. Greyfriars had palled at last. I had talked with Nelson and a friend of ours at home about socialism—somewhat to my surprise, they both declared themselves to be socialists—and Nelson was going out with a girl who called herself socialist (his engagement to Catharine had been broken off or, more accurately, had faded into thin air). I read all about socialism and the less boring bits of politics in the school library. I also happened on Keats and other poets—splendid fellows, I now discovered, who threw a few sidelights on what was happening between Virginia and me. In short, I was becoming civilised.

I was also working hard for School Cert. All that nightmare, the outward climax of one's school career, is so dead now that I have no intention of reviving it here. I passed it creditably, and that was the end of it. It was a bore at the time; it bores me now. Whereas Virginia still interests me.

It should not be imagined that the favourite school interest was dead to me. The cess-pit was still on the boil, as one might say. I now had the pleasure of finding that Brown slept only a few beds away from me in the dorm—to Webster's comic jealousy: 'I'll see they get *you*, old man, on that glorious day when the bloody revolution dawns!'

Brown had his adventure to relate. He claimed that in the holidays the gardener caught him trying to toss the family chow off in the asparagus patch, and had taken him into the potting shed, there inducing him to try the same tactics on what Brown described as a very large Hampden indeed.

Such tales, some true, some partially true, some wishful thinking, some downright lies, went the rounds at the start of every term; the lies sank and were forgotten, the truths survived and were welcome. Drury described how he had screwed his sister. We knew Drury screwed his sister; we had heard it from him before; he always came up with a wealth of detail, and there was not a boy did not envy him. Harper Junior claimed that his mother had got drunk and had sucked him off. We ignored Harper Junior.

I found I was growing secretive. Whereas, before this term, I had made much of my intentions towards Virginia—Sister Traven, as she again became during term—I now affected lack of interest in the whole matter, or I affected interest of a lewd and joking kind, to cover my real feelings. This acting role I had adopted at home, to protect myself from derision; it worked so well and for so long that I was eventually hard put to it to drop it, or even to determine my real feelings myself.

Similarly, I said nothing to anyone about Esmeralda, except once to Brown, when I told him he manipulated me almost as voluptuously as she did (for the knack of voluptuousness, or gift if it is that, never comes to some men or women; indeed, I believe it is a rarity, at least in northern Europe). Esmeralda and I had reached a truce, and a very agreeable one it was. We were both put off actually going all the way with each other, but on several occasions in the holidays we had got together and frigged each other in the friendliest way.

After her first burst of generosity in letting me have a good look at her fanny, Esmeralda was inclined to be much more frugal. 'It isn't supposed to be stared at,' she said.

I was, however, in a good bargaining position. Esmeralda wanted to see exactly how I worked.

Our favourite position was lying on our sides on her bed with Esmeralda behind me, looking over at my prick as she tossed it off, cunningly varying the pace, until I groaned and came into my outspread handkerchief. All this while, I had a hand clamped between her chubby legs. I would then roll her on to her back, make her spread wide her legs, and give her a reciprocal frigging.

She always came very quickly. The perfume of her private parts was beautiful to me; later in life, when I was more experienced, I would not have resisted the impulse to indulge my sense of taste as well as smell. At the time it was enough to enjoy her friendly animal company, and see her, satisfied, lie back and smile, and perhaps put a finger gently on her clitoris, to relish the last lingering feeling there.

Given the chance, I was a loving person. Sharing sexual experience with anyone always made me feel great affection for them; undoubtedly, I would have been absolutely crazy about Esmeralda, had it not been for the fateful attachment I felt for Sister. And I suppose a base general law was operating: Esmeralda had yielded, whereas Sister still promised. . . .

Only a few months earlier, the intimacies with Esmeralda would have been the peak of bliss. In many ways they still were; and for several days after term had begun I still kidded myself I could smell her blessed scent under one fingernail; but my love for Sister Traven was a higher peak.

Fortune sides with you if you give it a chance. My chance came early in the term. I was down to play with the first eleven against North Malverton, old rivals of ours. It was my first game in the first eleven, and I was conscious of the honour.

When the day came, I awoke feeling horribly ill. Whatever I had, it had been coming on for the two previous days. I told Page, the team captain, but he would not drop me. As long as I was on my feet, he preferred me to Bellarmine, who was twelfth man.

We fielded first. It was a hot day for May. I stood at square leg, and the field swam about me. I seemed to be talking to myself.

The Malverton captain—I forget his name now, but he had a moustache—had put himself to bat first. His score stood at forty-eight, and no wickets had fallen, when he hit the ball in my direction. I saw it coming, on its erratic course through the air, a nasty little red thing, growing, growing, eluding any attempt to catch it. It caught me smack on the forehead, above the left eye. They told me afterwards I made no attempt

to lift my hands to it at all. Field, cricketers, sky—
all spun away into blackness.

Rousing at last, I found myself lying in the sickroom. I was suffering not only from concussion
but from suspected pneumonia of the right lung.
The headmaster came to look at me, so I knew I
must be pretty bad. North Malverton won by
five wickets.

Sister Virginia Traven wore a white nursing
coat when she was on duty at school. Beneath it,
she liked the things in which I had seen her
during the holidays, clothes that women liked at
that time, a fawn woollen sweater, beneath which
the gentle contours of her breasts could barely be
distinguished (but I could distinguish them without any trouble), and a tweedy skirt. Over the
sweater she wore either a jacket that matched the
skirt or a rather shabby green suède jacket that
bore a Stockholm name-tab inside. Her stockings
and her shoes, which were soft, tan and 'sensible',
had no particular distinguishing mark. Her outfit
was, I suppose, almost exactly what was worn by
thousands of women of her class; but for me they
carried something of the glamour and mystery of
her elusive nature. I could have identified them
as hers among a parade of a thousand garments,
so firmly had I fixed their every particular

feature upon my brain. To come across her jacket lying discarded across the back of a chair was to experience a great feeling of poignance, of love, and of loss.

She was there unobtrusively in the sickroom that afternoon when I came to. She took my temperature and my pulse, standing by the bed. Later, she sat by me while the maid, Bovis, brought me a cup of tea. Inside my beating head everything external was remote, but her stillness came through to me.

Awful though I felt—I had a high temperature —I was full of light. I had been delivered into her hands. This was her lair, and she was in sole charge of me! Early in the summer term the sickroom was empty: no snivelling cases of flu or pink-eye, none of the mastoid cases of winter or the measles cases of spring. Just the bare room with flowers on the deep window-sill, while the other beds, hard as iron, created neat geometrical patterns round the walls.

As for its single occupant, I was something of a hero. I had gone on to the field against Malverton with pneumonia! The code of Branwells, ambivalent to suffering as to pleasure, decided it approved. A coal fire was lit in my room, although the weather was so fine. Bovis laid it and ceremoniously set light to it.

Fever made my first whole day's stay in the sickroom almost infinitely long. Lying and fret-

fully listening, the knock of bat against ball
reached me from evening nets practice. The air
was heavily pink with dusk as Sister made her
last rounds and Bovis brought me soup I did not
want.

When Sister had gone, when the great school
began to settle down for the night, and one by
one the whistling and stamping in the corridors
and the sounds echoing in the quad died into the
dark, I was left alone with my larking temperature. Hauling myself out of bed, I looked through
the window at the quad, deserted now except for
a master crossing it, smoking a pipe, carrying a
couple of books under his arm. The school
machine was functioning perfectly without me—
I, who might make head prefect next term. As I
realised how unimportant I was, an old loneliness
crept back, and I began to howl for comfort.

I howled for Esmeralda. In her arms I had had
most comfort.

Sister's room was situated above the sickroom.
She heard my cries and came down, shining a
torch. Her familiar clothes had gone; she was
no longer in uniform; she wore nightdress and
dressing-gown. Perhaps I had been crumpled on
the end of my bed longer than I thought; perhaps
I had howled less loudly and sustainedly than I
imagined—under the fever, my senses were distorted. Her first words to me were, 'Hush, it's
gone midnight! Everyone's asleep!'

Strange and thrilling words, quite conspiratorial!

She came up to me, felt my brow. I immediately clung to her. She was small and light, and was easily pulled on to the bed. I embraced her. Now I was crying, she was whispering excitedly to me.

That first love-making was a strange mixture of childish and adult fantasy—on both sides, no doubt. Virginia was partly mother-figure to me, and all the sweeter for that; while, at the same time, this was the first occasion on which I *loved* anyone, rather than simply rubbing genitals. I loved Virginia. I uncovered her little breasts and smothered them with wet kisses, I pulled back her flimsy clothes, I felt the beloved moisture between her narrow thighs, and we were united without effort. We lay side by side, rocking each other. It was all revelation!

She seemed to be whispering all the time; through the fever, I could not seem to register what she was saying. She called me by a strange loving name. And she needed me. Her need for me caught me unexpectedly, like a big wave, bathing me, lifting me. The vast stone school rose and circled round our heads. By the fugitive firelight, we were visible to each other only as amorphous shapes, my mythic lover and I.

Afterwards we lay there for a long time. My hand stroked her hair.

Finally, Virginia sat up. 'Virgin for short but not for long.' Modestly, she adjusted her clothes and set her hair right. I could make out that she was smiling at me, just as I lay beaming at her.

Many curious things occur to one that are almost beyond language to express. I have always liked women and been curious about them, possibly because my mother's temperament led me never to trust them entirely. With unidentified senses, I have always known a great deal about them, even when my experience of them was almost nil.

What I knew about Virginia may be put in one sentence: I knew that she was an intricate person, and yet with her goodness never far from the surface, and that in some way she had been deeply hurt, possibly beyond hope of redress. This intuitive knowledge illuminated her every gesture and word, investing them with an individual character, just as her clothes were invested with character.

This discovery that I could know women intimately (without allowing me to encroach on their privacy, for that my shyness did not allow) I insert here all too bluntly. At first, it seemed such a nebulous thing that I dared not trust it; only much later did I examine it carefully and find it not to be a beautiful delusion. But it must find a place here because I fell in love with darling Virginia, and that intuitive knowledge of something she could never tell me was one of the prime happy things then granted me.

Happily, self-reproach does not play a great part in my nature. My faults were early brought home to me; I have never lost them, or my deleterious habits. Yet they have never weighed too heavily because of my intimate knowledge that faults and weaknesses are essential components of everyone's nature. Perfection is only a pose of weakness.

This knowledge has permitted me to write as frankly as I have done here. It's a boyhood I describe, not a case history; to many who will not care to say so, my experiences will awaken resonances.

All I regret are my literary flaws, which will not permit me to relive here those early years. All I can do is to *re-tell* them, as honestly as possible, from the standpoint of age and memory.

Only at this point will I admit how inadequate my talent is to breathe life again into—to resurrect—that dear occasion when Virginia and I were complete and, for an indefinite span, all-in-all to one another.

'Now I'd better get my patient a cup of tea,' she said. Whatever she said was invested with a peculiar charm, a sort of irony, a sort of semi-official. . . . no, I can't describe it. It was not so much that she did not take herself or me or the world quite seriously, rather that she had a not-quite-serious policy to take nothing seriously.

Glutton that I was, as she started to leave the bed I reached out for her again.

'You're really very ill,' she said. But of course I was sure I would never in my life get her on the bed again.

Happily, it did not work out that way. Like the great A. K. Dancer before me, I had found love. Though it was still to be brought home to me that love, like everything else, has its flaws and weaknesses.

If it had been left to me, then, knowing no better, I would no doubt have conducted it as an affair of organs. But Virginia gently and slyly directed the affair on another course. She was not averse to sexual intercourse, but she insisted on social intercourse as well.

I was in the sickroom under her care and tutelege for fifteen days, fifteen flowering days. Not for ten years, until I made my wretched marriage, was I again to enjoy the company of a woman so exclusively and so continuously. In that time, without intending to, Virginia set her frail stamp upon me.

In that time the world stopped—though, in the last week, I had my school books and did some studying during the day. My friends came to see me and uttered rude and envious comments, at which I laughed and made coarse jokes back: made them against Virginia, lacerating myself as

I did so, in order that these uncouth sods, my chums, should not guess what was really happening.

One of them, a heavy-faced boy called Spaldine who came from Spalding and was also in the art club, was particularly pressing. I knew he fancied Virginia himself.

'You must at least have had a bit on a finger from her,' he said.

'For Christ's sake, you know I'd like to just as much as you would, Spaldine, you bastard, but if anyone touched her she'd go straight to the Head, and I'd be sacked before I knew it.'

'Go on, it would be worth it!' Spaldine said.

And they would leave, and my mysterious lover, twice my age, would come with her rapid walk into the room, seeming to behave for a moment as if our relationship were merely a formal one—as if she were perhaps as surprised by everything as I.

In the afternoons I was allowed to go up to her room, normally out of bounds, and sit on the sofa with her and even smoke a secret cigarette with her. We talked as equals. She liked to affect a drawl and speak very cynically, telling me amusing and sometimes risqué stories of her family, all of whom did interesting things. About herself she was more reticent.

The novelty and enchantment of all this filled every last corner of my life. I thought of her every moment I was awake, whether she was present or not; and she permeated my sleep, even when I did not dream of her.

Virginia's only drawback was that she was not as lecherous as I. Except for one occasion, she would not make love with me in the daytime. Evenings and nights, she said, were made for loving: bodies, becoming part of the darkness, were more sensuous then. I laughed and asked if her old Zulu had taught her that, but she said it was true. Perhaps it is.

Coupled with this belief of hers went a strong aversion to letting me see any part of her body unclothed. Her body, she said, was her secret; no one had ever seen it since she was grown up. Only after dark could I feel it and kiss it, and then in carefully circumscribed areas. She liked having her breasts kissed, but that was about the limit.

There was nothing wrong with her body; I could feel no scars. Recalling my secret knowledge that she had in some way been badly hurt, I asked her what unpleasant things had happened in her life.

'Nothing unpleasant ever happens to good girls, Horatio, darling.'

Later, however, she admitted that when her family had been living in Hong Kong, when she was a small girl and her father was stationed there, she had caught rheumatic fever, and only the extreme devotion of her mother's nursing had saved her.

Every night at midnight she came down to my bed in the sickroom. I argued that we would be safer from discovery in her room, for the duty master occasionally took it into his head to wander through the whole school; in addition, I wanted to savour for the first time the glamour of a female bed; but Virginia said that in the sickroom she could hear anyone coming in time to pretend she was simply on duty, whereas if we were up in her room, and my bed was found unoccupied, there would be a great row! So we lay together in love every time where we had first lain, and the thought that we could be caught perhaps added flavour to our happiness—for in some respects we were neither of us entirely unlike children playing a role.

Eventually, that role could be played on that stage no longer. My form master came to see Sister and asked pressingly that I be returned to school as soon as possible. I had to go. By this time I was perfectly fit, and Virginia was sending me out for long walks every day.

She had to sign me off, and I had to return to the school that had been waiting, sunlit, noisy, dusty, in the wings all this halcyon time. But she insisted that I was excused sport for another week and should continue to take my walks during that period.

Twice during those walks she met me at a pre-arranged spot. On one occasion she and I walked to Youlgreave and had hot toasted tea-cake and big cups of tea in a little whitewashed cottage that was still there, standing empty, during the war. I passed it on one drab occasion and recalled our bygone delight with a pang; for me it was a time of happiness at once placid and shot through with revelations. Despite her sophisticated background, Virginia seemed perfectly content with me, while every remark she let drop about the wider world she knew fascinated me.

It could not last. Once I was back in school, old embargoes snapped back into force. They were too strong to overcome. Both sickroom and her room were now out of bounds to me. I had no pretexts for meeting her, or she me. We could occasionally look at each other, but that shy evasive smile held no special message for me. Ah, my lost Virginia!

I cannot say love died. Indeed, it is not dead now. But I had to live as if it were dead. I had to work and play and laugh and swear. Brown jumped eagerly back into my bed again and we pulled each other off with almost the old abandon. Harper Junior, who had been growing obstreperous lately with the onset of puberty, was made to suck himself off by torchlight, in full disgraceful view of everyone. School life is school life. Reprieves are only reprieves.

The ordeal of School Cert came and was survived. Even at the time it seemed a dim and
academic exercise. As young men, we were fully
aware of the torches burning in Europe, and the
bayonets glinting and the crunch-crunch of
marching feet. We envied and hated the Hitler
Youth, with its general immorality (according to
the propaganda) and the willingness of the German maidens to bring forth children. We were
glad that—as yet—there was no war, but we
hated the peace.

Men aged twenty were already being con-
scripted into the forces; Britain was painfully
waking. An old boy, a colonel, came down and
talked to the school angrily about war. A recruiting poster appeared on the notice board. Hitler
and Mussolini made their Pact of Steel. We swam
in the green swimming-pool, and wanked and
exercised and waited for the invisible flags that
signal to young men.

As Hitler's Panzer divisions swept into Poland,
my stern old grandfather was felled by a stroke.
Nelson, my father, and I were sitting about use-
lessly in Grandfather's silent house when Neville
Chamberlain announced that Britain was now at
war with Germany. A few moments later our old
family doctor pronounced Grandfather dead.

'Just as well the old man never lived to hear
the worst,' Father said. He thought that war
would 'ruin everything'; and that was his dead

father's view also. Nelson and I looked speculatively at each other. I was two days past my seventeenth birthday. He, three years older, wore an incongruous army uniform. He had been called up two months before; this was his first forty-eight-hour leave. He and I had never seemed further apart; but he evidently understood what I was thinking, for he said, 'You can't join up yet!'

'You'll have to go back to school, Horatio,' Father said. 'You'll be perfectly safe at Branwells. The Germans will not be able to bomb us here.'

But I never went back to school again. Partly this was due to my parents; both were obsessed with how we could all be 'safe'; Father began building an enormous air-raid shelter in the garden, conscripting me to help with the digging and concrete-mixing. It seemed to me an extremely futile operation.

My chief reason for wishing never to see Branwells again, however, was entirely because of Virginia.

We met a few days after war was declared, when the country was quivering with an indecisive excitement. That excitement also ran through Virginia's slender frame. She had handed in her notice at Branwells and was going to join a nursing service! She hoped to go to France— she had old family friends in Paris.

This was—I must use the melodramatic old cliché which rang through my head at the time— the knell of doom. We were to be parted, perhaps for ever! I had hardly ever looked ahead. Inside our relationship I had been safe. The most I had imagined was that we should be together in the long summer holidays, that we might even swim in the river; or perhaps she and I might arrange to go down to the Hunstanton bungalow; or we would make love in one of the towers of Traven House. But now we were going to part for ever, and her darling tiny light would shine elsewhere! Paris! She might as well have said Mars!

Faced with the prospect of parting, I realised bitterly I was just a kid. How could I keep her? Or find her again once she had gone?

One thing at least was certain: those grey school buildings would be utterly intolerable without her dear transforming presence.

I broke down and wept, but later and alone, when the shock really hit me. When Virginia was beside me I met her news with schoolboy flippancy.

'Oh, you'll look so ducky in nursing uniform, Virginia, and all the men will go mad about you! I must see you in it at least once.'

'I don't want to drive you mad!'

'I am mad already. Before you go—Mother keeps asking me to ask you—come and have tea with us! Mother is anxious to see you again. And you'll see Ann—she's getting quite grown-up. She bought a lipstick at Woolworth's the other day, and puts it on when Mother is out.'

She sighed and looked down at her shoes.

'Do *you* want me to come to tea?'

'Not much. I mean, I shall be glad of the chance to see you, any old chance. But Mother can be a bit oppressive.'

'She doesn't think there's anything. . . . funny going on between us?'

I frowned at her. 'Funny? What's funny between us, Sister Traven? I'm dead serious, I don't know about you!'

In the end she agreed to come to tea that Friday. I have already given some account of that farewell feast.

When it was over, and I had driven with her to the cemetery, and she had gone, and I had dragged slowly back home to make another entry in my secret 'Virginia Journal', I lay for a long while on my bed, thinking about my life. Seldom had I so rigorously searched my soul; introspection was rare for me.

In those days I was incapable of seeing myself as essentially the ordinary fellow I now reluctantly conclude myself to be; I alternated between holding myself a great saint or a great sinner. One thing I did see: that, by what I then reckoned my own fault, I had failed to awake any real loving response in my parents. My brother and sister

loved me, and I was lucky in them; but theirs
was the slaphappy relationship of fellow nestlings
in the brood. I had become a rather isolated and
independent character. Sex, I told myself, had
taken the place of affection.

However, there was Virginia. Out of the sordid
chaos of school and my life in general, she had
provoked, inspired, the best love of which I was
capable. I wanted more of her love (even if she
didn't love me very greatly); and I wanted to
give her more. What had I ever given her, I, a
spotty youth?

A great emptiness filled me to think how un-
worthy I was.

With the emptiness, a stabbing knowledge:
she's left school now—the world's big—you will
lose sight of her any day—she's not so closely
tied to you, why should she be?—she could disappear without another word.

True! Within me, waiting for this opportunity
to reveal itself, lay more intuitive understanding
of this strange woman I loved. She was elusive to
me; and *so she was to herself*. Infinitely precious,
she could so easily be infinitely lost.

I almost broke out of my room in search of her
at that instant. Standing caged, I rested my forehead against my locked bedroom door.

I resolved to go and see her again next day. I
had to make some definite arrangement with her.
That was what we had never had. Never had I

shown her how deeply I cared; maybe I had been afraid to.

We had to have a proper relationship. After all, I was no longer a child. Neither of us was going back to Branwells. No longer need our love be clandestine. At last I saw the advantages of growing up!

That night brought me no sleep. I tried to read, could not; slipped down the drainpipe outside my window, walked to the outskirts of the town, came back, still could not rest. Eventually, tired and disgusted with myself, I took the usual way into oblivion and tossed myself off. Then I slept.

Next morning, her lovely face, half-mocking, was before me. While Mother told Father across the breakfast table everything Virginia had said at tea the previous day, I resolved that I must speak to Virginia—speak to her seriously.

Clear on what I had to do, I was muddled on how to do it.

Virginia's arrangements were slightly complicated. She had never wanted me to write to her at Traven House because one of the servants there pried into her affairs; I always wrote to an address in Nottingham, where she said she had some rooms. It was to this address that I resolved to go—it was accessible by train, whereas Traven

House stood miles off the map, and was too intimidating besides. I slipped away from home after lunch, pretending I was off for a game of cricket.

Such idiot plans court disaster. It was, really, my first set-back in the Virginia affair, and indirectly it may have helped me to stand apart from her.

The train chugged into Nottingham Midland Station by 2.30 and I set out on foot for Union Street. The name on paper always sounded so romantic: the union referred to was ours, hers and mine. The reality lay near the lunatic asylum and was extremely drab, a succession of terraced houses punctuated by shops in a semi-industrial area. My step faltered in dismay.

After much hesitation, hoping to run into her in the street, I went up to the number I had and rang the bell. After a while, a girl of about my age opened the door and peered out. She wore curlers in her hair, a pink apron, and fluffy pink slippers. From behind her came the cabbagey whiff of the house.

'Yes,' she said.

I asked politely for Sister Traven, making as if to walk in.

'That slut ain't in and she owes us rent!' And with that the bitch slammed the door in my face.

Shaken, horrified, doubting, I stood back. I was conscious of people looking at me from behind curtains.

What should I do? Post Virginia a note through the door? Knock again? Wait till someone else arrived at the house? In the end I did nothing. I walked to the end of the street, stood there with my hands in my pockets, and at last went away.

Everyone must experience such bitter reversals in love. Things happen which seem nothing to do with the quality of the human beings involved, glass-sharp nasty things that come grinding up out of the system in which mankind has to live, reminders of the horrid fact that we as humans must camp out as best we can among complex series of natural laws, which came into being long before man did, and so contain no provision for him or any finer feelings.

All I could do was return to the railway station. The one distraction was meeting Spaldine, then heading back for Spalding by train. He was as subdued as I was, having come over to Nottingham to volunteer for the R.A.F. We worked our way through a cup of vile coffee and a biscuit together in the station buffet before departing to our separate platforms. Strangely enough, the name of Sister Traven emerged in our conversation, but from a guarded question I put, I gathered that he knew nothing of her whereabouts.

Back home I went, empty-handed, empty-hearted. A certain ability for self-dramatisation may have eased the situation slightly. Nothing else did.

September wore on. At last my father wrote to the Head and said that he did not think any useful purpose would be served in sending me back to Branwells; I would be doing some war work until I was of an age to join the forces. The Head wrote back saying he entirely understood the position, that patriotism must come first, and that he required a term's fee in lieu of notice.

I was really alone. No, not really alone; Ann and I took to cycling off into the country with sandwiches for lunch. On one occasion Esmeralda came with us, but Ann and Esmeralda did not like each other—Esmeralda patronised her. We were completely isolated from our parents.

The old phantom idea of a war between generations is never far away in times when change makes the older generation appear obsolete instead of wise; for all that, it is a silly and distressing idea, in which both sides are losers. In 1939 that sense of division was particularly sharp.

My father volunteered for the Navy, in which he had served in the Great War (as he called it). He was turned down because he was too old. His generation was suddenly faced with the fact that they were 'past it'. It was a generation, too, which thought of the new war in terms of the old. To men like my father, the war promised to be merely a stale repetition of the horrors of the previous conflict.

For 'Uncle' Jim Anderson, the war took on a different aspect. I have mentioned this occasional visitor to our house. Nelson and I always suspected that there was 'something going on' between him and Mother. In the last days of that September everyone was changing, every relationship was changing; and 'Uncle' Jim, that uncertain man, was changing with the times.

He turned up one afternoon when Ann was at school, Father at the bank, and Mother on one of her walks. To my irritation, I had to make conversation to him. He marched about our living room in the smart walking-out uniform of an infantry regiment; and my irritation was partly with myself for being impressed.

In a short while, as he talked, it dawned on me that he was not just talking to kill time until my mother returned, but was genuinely trying to communicate with me. I was too sunk into myself to respond; and I can have paid little attention to him, for, even a brief time afterwards, I could not recollect what he spoke about, except that it was serious, and that he ended by saying, referring to the war, 'I've wasted away my life so far—perhaps now I shall be able to make something of it!'

When he said goodbye to my mother she turned pale and ran upstairs.

Into everyone's stagnant lives a current was circulating.

To us who were young, the air was vibrant with hopes and threats. The black on the map, by which Germany was represented, was a thrilling incarnation of evil, to which we were drawn despite ourselves. It represented a sort of liberty.

I tried to volunteer for service. I was turned down. The British Government had called up the eighteens to the forty-ones, and its hands were full organising them. Looking back, I see it was typical of the Stubbs family that both Father and I should volunteer within a few days of each other—rather than go together and meet our rebuffs together!

Then came word from Virginia.

Sick and unsettled, I was desperately glad to hear anything. Her letter was written in her untidy scribble ('that upper-class scrawl', as I admiringly thought of it) on violet notepaper.

She said she had joined the Q.A.I.M.N.S. (or Q.A.R.A.N.C., as it now is). She was staying in London, in the Queensway district, with an old friend who was currently making a name for herself in a West End stage play; life was quite pleasant despite the war. She hoped I would come and see her some day before I went back to school.

Everything in that note made me at once happy and miserable. The greatest vexation was that its tone was only lightly affectionate—oh, Virginia's tone to the life, as I realised, but what I wanted was meaty, heart-baring declarations of love!

And that bit about 'hoping you'll come and see me' . . . She knew I had been to London only three or four times in my life, when Mother took Nelson and me down for a treat. Of course, I was gratified that Virginia asked me at all. . . . but then there was the jibe, as I saw it, about being a schoolboy, which I no longer was.

Nor did she mention the three letters I had written to her c/o Union Street. Had she never received them? Had the young harridan grabbed them first, or had Virginia not bothered to read them? Or preferred to ignore them?

All of a sudden, my blood growing decidedly chilly, I decided that I would go down to London and see her. I would get a job near her. I could see her every day then. I would leave home. Nobody would care.

My mind was made up: I carried my resolution through. Although I have called myself timid, I have portrayed myself as acting boldly on several occasions. The two are not incompatible.

One of the mainsprings of my nature—which I was then trying ineffectually to understand—was a deep inferiority complex caused, as an anxious reading of the psycho-analytical shelf at the public library informed me, by my apparent rejection by my parents. When I once decided to do a thing I could only go through with it with the doggedness of a weak man—often to arrive at accomplishment without the wind in my sails to go further and press home the advantage I had gained. Until I grew beyond this stage I let myself in for many disappointments which cumulatively allowed me no chance to think well of my management of my own insignificant life.

Before I left home I went to say goodbye to Esmeralda. She and her mother were now alone in the big house. Esmeralda's father had paraded through the town in dashing infantry dress uniform and then driven off to join his regiment. Esmeralda's mother might have been alone, but she was not lonely; she made it clear that officers were welcome at her house provided they came in small parties and left in the same way. I heard Mother telling Father that she was no better than she should be; they were not keen that I should see Esmeralda, but by now I was somewhat independent and they did not like to issue direct orders in case they were disobeyed directly.

When I arrived at Esmeralda's house a gramophone was playing. This was the fag-end of September. By now Brown would be up to his spunk-producing tricks in the dormitory, and the British Expeditionary Force was almost ready to move into France. Perhaps some of the officers present that night were due to go. Their presence only helped my schemes, because Esmeralda was sitting upstairs in her bedroom, rather sulky. Her mother did not want her downstairs—though she was all dressed up to go in and kill, given half a chance. She told me she liked kissing officers.

Dramatically, I told her that she could kiss all the officers she liked. I could no longer allow myself to feel jealous of what she did: I was off to London, and was going to join the war as soon as I could.

She had the grace to be prettily sad about this. We started kissing. Down below, the gramophone was playing 'Doing the Lambeth Walk!' and 'Where's That Tiger?'. We were all absolutely vulnerable to the passage of time.

Was it the music or the occasion? Suddenly I had a wild impulse. She had her little warm hand in my flies, but I broke away.

I began to confess to Esmeralda all the sexual stunts at school—not a word about Virginia, of course, but everything about the boys, and how Branwells was really nothing but a huge brothel. She sat there, staring at me. Once I started, I could not stop.

To this day, I do not know what provoked the confession. But the very word confession suggests that I laboured under a feeling of guilt for what had gone on. If so, this was not conscious. Nelson and I were lucky in that Father never lectured us on the perils of masturbation; he was far too reserved to do so. As I have said, I never suffered from the fears of blindness or backache or stunted growth with which some Branwells boys were afflicted. Partington—he who took so long to reach orgasm—told me once that his father lectured to him for an hour about it, made him uncover his cock, told him to read the Bible when he felt lust coming on; and Partington took the advice to heart so literally that on one occasion he had enclosed his rampant, sin-bound organ within the delicious India-paper pages of the Holy Book and frigged himself with it until he shot his roe in the middle of the Prophet Isaiah. He suffered miseries for that blasphemous act. Whereas I—who never looked on any sexual exercise as other than the use of organs there for the purpose—I never suffered mental or physical trouble on any occasion.

Perhaps my confession had a simpler prompting. Perhaps I just wished to be free of the shadow of public-school life for ever.

And perhaps I also hoped to make Esmeralda sexier than usual by telling her a spicy tale.

She was certainly interested. Trying to get similar confessions from her, I asked her if she had not done similar things and had similar things done to her.

'Not by other girls! Girls don't do such things!'

'They do! They are called lesbians, after a famous Greek woman who used to do it.'

'Greek women, perhaps! But not English girls!'

'But you sometimes do it to yourself, Esmeralda, don't you?'

'Well. . . . that would be telling, wouldn't it?'

'How often?'

'Don't ask rude questions! How often do you do it?'

'About once a week.' I daren't tell her the truth.

'Let me see you do it!'

We had an argument about that. I was willing but shy, and needed to be talked into it. Eventually, I brought out my penis, which was well inflated by all the discussion, and began to rub it, on the understanding that she would finish for me. There was a perverse and unexpected delight in doing it boldly in front of her, and thus perhaps breaking down a barrier in her mind as well as my own. So I did it slowly and lasciviously, pulling down my pants at the same time, so that she could see me naked, and my balls and everything.

Esmeralda began to tremble. Her eyes gleamed, her lips parted. Her hand stole up her skirt as if without her knowledge, and at the sight of it, I came in a swoon, sending the semen scattering over her carpet. She was annoyed and excited. I was still excited myself. We began kissing violently. With her help, I eased down her knickers and commenced to frig her wet and slopping little organ. Insensibly, it changed to fucking, and she was oh-ing and ah-ing feverishly. This was the first time I had gone into her. It was the greatest delight to thrust into her just as far as I could get. Downstairs, the gramophone was pounding, and she flopped back gasping under me. The movement dislodged me—just as well, because as I came out, all red and be-juiced, the orgasm was on me and I pumped my roe against her chubby thighs.

'Oh,' she said, and we just lay there. 'Oh God!'

After a bit she took hold of my little limp organ and kissed me on the lips. She slid her tongue into my mouth, starting very slowly to massage life back into the sausage in her clutch.

Into my ear she whispered hotly, 'You told me one of those boys did it to you three times straight off. Now your sexy Esmeralda is going to do it to you three times straight off, and I won't take no for an answer!'

She was, I'm happy to say, as good as her word.

Leaving home was more taxing than I had expected. The truth was, I still loved my mother dearly; her inability to understand anything about the way I thought or felt had caused me to build a layer of indifference over my feelings for her. But when she wept as I went and said she did not know what to do without me now that both her boys had forsaken her, I was deeply mortified and disturbed to think that I had been unfair to her.

Home was sadly depleted. Ann now had a boy friend of her own, a younger brother of my old enemy Barrett. She clung to me and wept before I left; childhood was ending for her too. We no longer had a maid living in; Beatrice was married and came only in the mornings from 8.30 to one. My father was coping with increasing regulations and dwindling staff at the bank.

Filled with mixed emotion, I went and loitered about by the bank on one of those last evenings, hoping to say something to Father that would enable him to speak to me in the way I always knew he could.

Although it was daylight yet in the street, a light burned in the bank; above the frosted section of the glass I could occasionally see father's head and that of the chief cashier. I recalled the times when I had stood here as a small boy, waiting for him to come out, check the door to see that it was securely locked behind him, take my hand, and lead me home. That was no more expected. Now I was grown up, and he might like me better if I behaved like a man.

The chief clerk came out of the side door. I hid round the corner so that I did not have to speak to him. I went back to the side door of the bank, standing there smiling as my father came out.

'Hello, Dad!'

'Hello, Horatio! What are you doing here? Are you waiting for me?'

With an effort—'Yes, Dad, I was, really. I thought perhaps we could—well, you know I'm off on Friday—I thought perhaps we could go and, you know, have a sort of farewell drink!'

'A drink?' He frowned at me, not at all unkindly. 'Here, you'd better come home with me. What do you want a drink for? At your age! I don't want you hanging about the public houses and I hope you won't when you're in London.'

'No, I won't, Dad.'

'Well, I don't want a son of mine seen in a pub. I know Nelson has been in one a time or two, but we hope he'll grow out of that. You know your mother's upset enough at your going to London— I don't know what she'd do if she thought you were going into public houses. It's the downward road, my boy, make no mistake of that.'

'Yes, Father.'

'There's a good lad! Let's see if she's got something nice for my tea.'

I thought at the time how damned nice he was, and how uncouth and depraved I must have seemed, trying to get him to go for a drink; as far as I knew, he had never seen the inside of a pub. And as a bank manager he had a position to keep up. What made Father seem all the more mild and restrained was that he should make only oblique reference to a squabble of the previous month, when Nelson had actually taken me into a country-type pub just on the outskirts of town; we had each smoked a fag and drunk a half-pint of shandy—and on emerging into the guilty light of day had been spotted by one of the bank's prosperous customers and reported. Father was extremely angry on that occasion (the customer had been Mr. Tansley-Smith), and Nelson and I had had a lecture about the evils of drink and the sort of company we were likely to meet in such disgraceful haunts as 'The Three Feathers'.

So that was it. When it came time for me to get my London train, Father said no more about 'The Three Feathers' episode, or about my strange invitation to him, and we parted with a good affectionate handshake; but I could only feel he expected that no good would come of me in London and would hold out no great hopes for my future.

Mother, at the last moment, appeared more perky.

'It's a shame you should be leaving me so soon, darling! You're so young!'

'I've been going away to school for years, though, haven't I?'

'That's different! Still, I suppose you will be able to look after yourself—if you find a good landlady. Why, she'll probably love to have a boy of your age to mother! She'll spoil you! And perhaps she'll ask your poor old mother down to stay, one day! And you will write every week, won't you? Nice long letters?'

It all seemed like an anticlimax. At one time I had imagined that Nelson, Ann and I would stage a sort of absolutely bloody little revolution of our own and march out of the house *en masse*. But we left one by one, going forth from the paternal roof as much in bewilderment as revolt, reluctantly rather than grandly.

London was also not as I had imagined it; my arrival was hardly triumphal. But I soon found lodgings in a gaunt little house standing at the extreme north end of Queensway, where I rented a gaunt little room under the roof. The tenants were a Mr. and Mrs. Stevenson—Wilf and Lou, as they soon became. I rarely saw Wilf; he had a night job, maintenance man on the Underground, but his wife was kind to me and fed me well, although she was in other respects a rather mean woman. I did not greatly mind. I had other interests.

First among these must be counted the thrill of being in London. That great city was then at one of its historical turning points. As I look back to that autumn and winter of 1939 now, I see a city of long ago, ruled by men who were essentially Victorian, inhabited in its less fashionable thoroughfares by people who held many of the beliefs of the Victorian Age, and who lived among the relics of that age. It was a city which, despite the First World War, had peace built into it and so was able to turn only reluctantly and face the angry dawns of war.

But that very effort had stirred it up. You knew that something was happening in London, a sort of psychic earthquake. Out of the massed villages that together constitute the capital, people were slipping; and, as unobtrusively, new people were slipping in, like rowboats passing unnoticed under Tower Bridge, bringing dynamite. Signs of war were apparent. Barrage balloons hung here and there. Adhesive paper criss-crossed on windows. Sandbags were up. The city was getting secret. It was after dark that the subversive aspects became most apparent. In the blackout, London hummed like the larger version of the dormitories of Branwells that it was. I was too young to realise that yet, for I had still to find my way around; but I certainly picked up the tension on my highly tuned antennae.

I had no trouble in getting a job in one of the ministerial departments now rapidly springing up everywhere. I chose it not only because it was just round the corner from Lou Stevenson's, but because it was housed in a gigantic building and had a STAFF VACANCIES notice on the door, as well as an attractive air of mystery in its seedy porch.

My duties were both light and nebulous, consisting almost entirely of sorting an endless stack of file cards into two packs: those bearing the names of males and those bearing the names of females; and then shuffling the female pack into alphabetical order. Half the women in the British Isles must have slipped through my fingers.

One morning, as I was leaving Lou's for the department, a letter arrived for me bearing Virginia's 'aristocratic scrawl' on the envelope. I opened it and read it—a glance sufficed to do that—as I emerged among the pedestrians in the grey and sooty Bishop's Bridge Road.

The thought of Virginia had never been far from me. On my first day in London, as soon as I had found a room and taken my few possessions from my papier-maché suitcase, I sat on the bed and wrote to her, giving her my address, announcing dramatically my arrival in the metropolis. I could not resist telling her that I had come especially to find her; although I declared that I loved her, I was careful to add that I would not make myself a nuisance to her; I longed only to see her as soon as possible.

It was eleven long days later that her answer arrived, to be ripped open in the Bishop's Bridge Road. With what I told myself was facile despair,

I had begun to assure myself that she would never reply: she had done just as I feared and vanished into the great hazy quicksands of the world.

Virginia's tone in her note lay somewhere between guarded and chilly. She simply invited me to come and see her at 8.10 on the following night. Her letter offered at least an implied explanation for her delay in answering; her address was now in Lansdowne Lane.

At seventeen, all love's weather is heavy. As I sorted my filing cards, I thought I would say to her bravely, before she could speak, 'I know you have ceased to care about me; I am too proud to bother you further'; and I would turn and lose my way for ever in the dark streets of the capital. Or at another moment, I thought—well, it is immaterial now what I thought, all those years ago. All day I worked away at my trestle table, wondering at how a letter like mine could be answered by a letter like hers; for I had yet to grasp the simple principle that adults finally and sadly have to grasp, that people follow their own behaviour which they are not necessarily able to alter for anyone else. Only the immature can throw up everything and begin anew.

I had to question several people in the department before I discovered how to find her address. 'It's somewhere off Holland Park Avenue,' I was told.

Those were hungry days; I was always short of cash. On the next evening I left work, went back to my room to wash and spruce myself up, watering down my hair and all that, and then returned to the streets, passing the department again to get to a little pie-and-peas shop I had found. The pies were cheap and good. With luck, with will-power, I could make that meal my tea and supper; on a bad day, and they came fairly frequently, I would be forced by the thought of closing time to burst out of my room again later in the evening, to seek another last bite to eat.

Full of pie, I headed towards Notting Hill and Virginia. Now I worried chiefly over the precision of Virginia's timing, as implied in her letter. She wished me to appear at 8.10. Exactly what was the nicety of her arrangements that eight should be too early for her and 8.15 presumably too late?

My morale—a word we were then beginning to hear frequently—had sunk still lower by the time I reached Virginia's address; the several wrong turnings I had taken, my base hesitancy in approaching strangers to ask the correct way, had convinced me that I was destined always to take life's wrong turnings. Now, there I was, forty-three minutes early, if my watch was correct—and even that could not be relied upon. Rain was falling. I wore my mac, since that happened to be the only outside garment I possessed.

The house in which Virginia lived was one of a long terrace of a kind prevalent in that area of London: three storeys high plus basement, with would-be-grand steps leading up to the front door under pretentious porches. Once these had been the residences of prosperous middle-class families; by the war they were already subdivided and mysterious people came and went by private doors. Nowadays they are still further divided, and the roof which once sheltered my frail Virginia now keeps the rain off a large family of solid and stern-faced blacks.

I stood under a porch from which I might survey Virginia's porch and detested my hopes and fears.

At 8.08 I shovelled my thoughts back into place and went over and rang at Virginia's bell.

A man, smiling and suave and of call-up age, confronted me, nodding and grinning even more widely as I declared whom I was after, but without actually speaking, which transformed his smiles into gems of hostility. He waved me into the hall, put his hands abruptly in his pockets, and led me upstairs, leaving me outside a door on the first floor. I tapped and went in, hating every moment.

Virginia was sitting on the sofa, smoking, wearing her customary clothes and wry expression. Sitting in an armchair was another girl of about the same age, also smoking. The room was drab; a black paper blackout dominated the room. In the hearth a small electric fire burned; over the mantelpiece was a coloured print of a man sitting on a horse in a condition print dealers refer to as 'somewhat foxed'. The only thing that heartened me was the sight of one of Virginia's dabby landscape sketches on a side wall.

'Hello, Horatio! What fun seeing you down in the wicked city! Rather different from the wilds of Derbyshire! Say hello to my friend Josie. She lives here.'

I said hello to Josie, and went and sat by Virginia. I got up and took my mac off without being asked. I sat down again by Virginia; she smiled quickly and looked away from me. Her face was thin and rather lined; for the first time I realised she was really pretty old, older than she claimed to be. She offered me a cigarette from the open packet on the sofa arm.

'How's life in the Nursing Service?' I asked diffidently.

'I haven't joined yet. A friend of mine is trying to get me a good position.' Or perhaps she said commission.

'I thought you said you had joined.'

'I'm hoping to join next week.'

Conversation died. I waited for Josie to go.

She lit another cigarette, examining it with intense curiosity between puffs.

'Look, Virginia, I'd naturally like to talk to you privately, if I could.'

It turned out this was Josie's flat. Virginia was just looking round for a flat of her own. She had left her last one because the landlady was so horrid. Desperately, I asked her to come round to my place; it wasn't far; we could walk. She said she did not want to go out; she was expecting someone to come and see her in a little while. I pressed her harder. She and Josie looked at each other, she nodded and led me into the adjoining bedroom.

The room was only dimly lit, but I observed that it was small and extremely untidy. Clothes hung everywhere. I clutched her and told her I loved her, needed her desperately, had come to London just to be near her. She put her arms round my neck and looked up at me, half-smiling, still taking nothing seriously. She started talking about Josie, who was in love with a captain in artillery, but I cut her off. I asked if she was in some sort of trouble.

'There is some trouble, Horatio, darling, but I would advise you to keep out of it. It's grown-ups' trouble, not for boys.'

'Thanks, Virginia, but I am grown up or I wouldn't *be* here.'

She frowned as if I had said something in-

[156]

comprehensible and continued, 'The trouble is my cousin, a very bad cousin—I forget if I told you about him. You know my mother was an invalid for years. She died recently and there is some terrible trouble about the will—a lot of money is involved. My cousin is trying to get hold of it. I have to be very careful.'

'Was that your cousin who showed me up here? The smarmy chap?'

'That's a cousin of Josie's, and he's really awfully jolly.'

She started telling me about him and what he was doing, and what other people who lived in the house were doing. By refraining from interrupting, I gained time with her, and time to try to adjust to the sensation I had that she was at once as she had always been and yet also entirely changed—a dual feeling that radiated from my mysterious intuitive source. Too restless to listen properly to what she was saying, I prowled about the encumbered room, dragging at my cigarette. There were several ashtrays in the room, most of them full of ash and stubs. By the side of one of the two single beds, a book lay open, face down; that was a habit of Virginia's. It was a novel of Ethel Mannin's, *Venetian Blinds*; by chance, I had recently read it myself and thought it rather daring. I stared down at it, trying to make it provide me with a clue to Virginia's mood, and over my head flew details of strange lives, people getting exotic war jobs, mysterious and handsome refugees from Hungary, husbands and wives changing into uniform. In between all this, Virginia dropped only the most stray word about herself.

It was an infuriating meeting. I could not piece together what was happening. She seemed unable to explain properly, or to make up her mind. It even appeared to me that she was lying about intending to join the Q.A.I.M.S. I begged her to meet me at the British Museum, so that we could spend some time together and go somewhere where we could walk and talk. Eventually she gave me a kiss and said she would drop me a note. I had to insist that she wrote down my address and did not just rely on her memory; doing that entailed going back into the other room and borrowing a little diary pencil from Josie. Josie was still smoking in her armchair.

Virginia came out on to the landing, still smiling rather anxiously, glancing at her watch. We kissed goodbye, and I went down the dim stairs in a muddle of emotion.

I let myself out into the street. By now it was absolutely dark and raining slightly; my sense of time and place was disoriented. I stood for a moment and then started off along the pavement. Such was my misery that when I heard someone walking close behind I did not bother to look round. I turned a corner and as I did so my shoulder was grabbed. Turning, I was hit inaccurately in the chest.

The blow caught me off balance and I fell over. My attacker began kicking me. I grasped his legs, dragged him down, and reached out for his throat. He was about my size, by the feel of things. He was hitting me in the face, and we rolled into the gutter. Terror and anger seized me. He wore a slippery mac, buttoned up round the throat, so that I could not hold him properly. I banged his head on the road. He struggled away but I had hold of him.

A car passed down the road. By the dimmed light of its headlamps, I saw the man I was fighting with.

'Spaldine!' I exclaimed. I let go of him and he began running. But I ran after him and called his name again. He stopped and we confronted one another, fists clenched, in the middle of the roadway.

'Oh, my Christ! Stubbs!' he gasped.

We went into a little pub, mopped ourselves up in the Gents', and then sat at a table and talked over half-pints of bitter and cigarettes.

Spaldine was full of jealousy and bile. Once he started the tale of his grievances, he could not stop. And the target of his love and hatred was

Sister Traven—as he called her throughout his account.

He had first made love to Sister at Branwells about three weeks before I did. He had been entirely more precipitate than I. He had gone up to her room sometimes in the early hours of the morning and had stayed till dawn. He was crazy about her.

No coherent feelings, apart perhaps from amazement at my own pain, came to me as he talked. Although I interjected remarks, and they came from numbed lips, they were innocuous remarks that apparently rendered him quite insensible to any effect he was having on me.

'What about Pepper? He was the prefect in your dormitory. Didn't he ever find you were missing?'

'I always went up to Sister Traven's room in my pyjamas and dressing-gown. Then if I met anyone I could say I was feeling sick, see? Pepper, he used to sleep till the Five-to Bell! From Sister's room you can hear old Scrimbleshanks going across the quad to ring the Rising Bell. That was the signal for me to leave her. She never wanted me to leave her.'

'Nobody ever caught you getting back to dorm?'

'You can always make excuses, can't you, Stubbs? Been for a shit, or something.'

That he could equate that with lying with Virginia!

Forgetting his anger, Spaldine began telling me some of the stories of her earlier life which I had heard. But there were alarming little differences between his accounts and the ones I had received, the only one of which I remember was that she told Spaldine (later in their relationship, this was) that when her family was living in Tanganyika she and her sister had been pursued by hornets and had had to jump into a lake with all their clothes on to avoid the insects. It was a distorted echo from my own life, coming back to me disturbingly now.

Spaldine had soon begun to guess that Sister was taking other lovers. At one time he suspected me, but his brief conversation with me in the sickroom had deflected his suspicions; frankly, he said, he regarded me as too yellow to try any such thing. So he had kept watch elsewhere.

'Do you mean to say you deliberately spied on her?'

'I wasn't going to let anyone else get up her if I could help it, was I?'

'Weren't you?' Several lifetimes of hatred drifted between us, mine only mitigated by sorrow for poor innocent Virginia, who had somehow been cozened into taking this lout into her bed. As I looked at the blunt and detestable features of the lout, I recalled how this was the fellow who used to toss himself off and press his fingers against the base of his beastly prick, so as to save

[161]

his beastly semen; had he told *her* that, I wondered?

Hating to hear every word, I nevertheless needed to hear more, as if the poison never poisoned enough. Interrupting him curtly, I went and bought two more half-pints, thinking that that put paid to pie-and-peas for the next day.

When I set his drink in front of him he lifted the glass and sipped without a word of thanks, frowning, still involved with his hateful story.

Watching Sister became his obsession, and soon he found confirmation of his suspicions.

'Who do you reckon was getting stuck across her? I'll tell you! Angel-Face Knowles!'

'Knowles! No! He was just a kid!'

'He was getting stuck across her, I tell you, slimy little bastard!'

Knowles could only have been fifteen. Knowles' parents were extremely rich. Knowles managed to hire a car from the village; he met Sister at a prearranged spot, and they were driven away somewhere—Spaldine never managed to find out where, but he saw them drive off in the general direction of Derby. He tackled Knowles about it later.

Apparently Knowles was eager to boast of his escapade. He said they had checked into a hotel and he had been registered as Sister's son! I had no means of knowing whether this happened, or whether it was a fantasy of Knowles's or of

Spaldine's. Spaldine was revealing himself as a highly unbalanced character.

He had threatened to report Knowles to the Head; Knowles, a cool customer, dared him to do it. Spaldine then hit him, and Knowles promised that if another blow landed then *he* would go to the Head and make his report on Spaldine. Checkmate.

Knowles lived over in Cheshire, so Spaldine at least had the holidays clear, as he imagined. He could think about nothing but Sister—his family considered him mad. He decided he must cycle over to Traven House to see her.

Another revelation was coming. I saw it in his eyes. My stomach was chilled with beer and anguish. I had to excuse myself and go into the Gents' for a pee. As I stood there, I was saying to myself, half-aloud, 'What's he going to say next? What's he going to say next?'

When I got back to the table Spaldine had craftily lit a fresh cigarette, thus saving himself the necessity of offering me one. He blew smoke out across the table and said, 'You never went to Traven House, did you?'

'I *was* going, but we changed our plans.'

'Like that, was it? Give over, Stubbs. I know who changed the plans! She did—she had to! She doesn't live at Traven House any more than I do.'

'You're lying, Spaldine!'

'Look, I turned up there about twelve o'clock. Great big house all going to pot, it is! An old man answered the door, some sort of a butler, I suppose. I asked for Sister and the old boy said there was nobody of that name there, very poker-faced. Of course, I said I knew better. They'd got birds nesting under the porch affair. I kicked up a bit of a fuss. The old bloke started shouting. Eventually a chap calling himself Captain Traven turned up. He could have been sixty or seventy, I suppose. Anyhow, he sent the aged retainer away and tried to sort things out a bit. I told him why I was there, and he asked me in for a beer. He was civil enough—he'd been in the Army, he said. Walked with a limp. It was a funny house, a lot of sporting what's-its on the walls. As I say, he gave me a beer. I needed it. And we had a chat. They'd got a kind of a billiard room there.'

'What relation was this captain to Virginia?'

From what Spaldine said, I gathered that the captain squeezed more information out of Spaldine than Spaldine squeezed out of him. The captain sounded a shady character, the way Spaldine told it, but a few words from Spaldine could have made the Archbishop of Canterbury sound like a cheap crook.

The captain had evaded Spaldine's question about Virginia, much as Spaldine evaded mine about her. He had talked about the failure of business interests. A hag-like woman with dyed red hair had appeared, lit a cigarette, and inspected Spaldine; she asked him if he was staying for lunch (to which the captain had sharply said 'No'), and then drifted off without another word; Spaldine said he was willing to bet that the hag was not the captain's wife.

'What did he say about Virginia?'

Spaldine had led the conversation round to Virginia, and the captain told him that she was his daughter—his only daughter; after his second marriage she had become very difficult; eventually she had left under a cloud—this many moons ago, Spaldine gathered—with mutual vows that she would never return. She had tried to set the house on fire.

The repulsiveness of this story owed much to the obnoxious character of the man who was telling it, but it had certain features in its own right that exercised very little appeal on me. Even supposing Spaldine had inserted no lies of his own into the account, there was no telling how much of the story was a fabrication of the captain's. Spaldine had said of him, by way of description, that he wore 'a sort of military dressing-gown'; and somehow this detail alone was enough to conjure up in my eyes a whole career of unscrupulousness. I felt myself close to the dusty source of that terrible ill which I always knew had been done Virginia at some period in the past.

No such reflections detained Spaldine. He was pressing on with his tale of disenchantment.

Still on the trail of Sister—and now more savagely than ever, I gathered—he had cycled in to Nottingham and hammered on the door in Union Street. The slut (described by Spaldine as 'a little honey in sexy pink slippers') had opened up to him and shown him Virginia's room upstairs. Virginia was in, and alarmed to see him. He was furious and created a big scene, during which she wept. Later she soothed him and said that even if her situation was not quite as she had represented it, it was certainly not as her father had represented it. He was a cruel man who had turned out her and her mother, so that he might live in sin with the red-haired woman. He was currently trying to disinherit her from the money due to her in her grandfather's will.

All the time Spaldine raved on about the lies Sister had told him and the damage she had done him, I was aware how my hatred of him was growing. He referred to her as a snake-in-the-grass, using the expression several times, but he was my snake-in-the-grass; plainly, he had bullied Virginia, and had still been screwing her in Union Street, even when he had begun, by his own admission, to hate her. To think I'd met him in Nottingham, that very day, shortly after he had been seeing her, had bought him a cup of coffee, had never suspected a thing!

How I felt about Virginia was another matter. I was then unsure how I felt; an immense lake of sorrow was growing inside me, but partly it was because I regretted she had become involved with Spaldine.

However, it was clear that many of Spaldine's charges against her were correct in essence. Virginia had deceived everyone. The wealthy upper-class background she had sketched was a myth—as I should have seen, had I had more experience, from her worn clothes and the shabby rooms in which she had to live.

'You realise that the bitch is even now having it off with somebody else?' Spaldine said. 'She came down here because she couldn't get enough round Nottingham.'

'She's allowed to choose, isn't she?'

'Don't give me that stuff! She's got an obligation to me—to us, let's say, hasn't she? To me, anyhow. Just because she was sacked from school. . . .'

'What? She was sacked? Are you sure? She never told me she was sacked!'

'She never told you a bloody thing, Stubbs!'

'She told me she wanted to join the Nursing Service.'

'Oh, did she! She told *me* she had to come to London to act as principal witness in some involved divorce case concerning a friend.'

'Well, she mentioned that to me too—perhaps both are true.'

[167]

'Look, they're neither true, you silly clot! I reckon she got bunked!'

'You've no proof?'

'I reckon the Head found out what she was up to. Christ, man, she must have had half the Upper School across her at one time or another. Someone on the staff would have been bound to find out!'

'You're just guessing, and you've no right to say that. I don't see you've got any right to watch her house, either—much less clobber anyone who comes out.'

He shambled up to the bar and bought two more half-pints of beer and a packet of Woodbines. I watched him and saw what a radically unattractive fellow he was, his fair hair standing up in spikes, his nose pudgy and dismal and his trousers filthy from our scramble. No doubt I looked as bad myself. The knuckles of my left hand were bleeding badly, and I had wrapped them in a dirty handkerchief. Two sordid young men of seventeen, Virginia's lovers! Poor dear Virginia!

Spaldine put the beer down and lit a fag. I cadged one off him. A couple of old women were watching us covertly, attracted by Spaldine's vehement manner, doubtless. I gave them a good hard stare, mean-mouthed, and they looked away.

'See, something fishy's going on round at hers,'

Spaldine said. 'I bloody know there's some other bloke having it off with her. She put me off meeting her tonight, you know. She doesn't want me any more, that's for sure!'

'Wouldn't it be better to resign yourself to the worst? You can't make her' (I gulped) 'love you.'

'Are you bloody daft? Look, what I thought we'd do is this. We can have a plan of action, see? With two of us it's easy. We take it in turn to watch her place. She generally goes out in the morning. Instead of following her, we could slip in there and one search her room while the other kept look-out. Then we could find this other bloke's name and address. . . .'

'No! Spaldine, try and see this from a sensible angle. . . .'

'No, listen, you don't know what I was going to say!'

'I don't want. . . .'

'Listen, never mind that! I wasn't going to say we should go and beat him up. I reckon perhaps I was wrong there. Wrong tactics! We go round and see this other bloke and just *scare him off*, you see!' He delivered this looking at me hard, his eyes blazing with inspiration, watching to see the delight dawn on my face as I took in the brilliance of his plan.

'Balls!' I said.

'No, don't you see. . . . Look, we can act a bit

tough with him to show him we can't be mucked about. But we tell him, just tell him, all about the downright lies Sister has told us. That should scare him off.'

'Why? Has it scared you off, Spaldine?'

He looked away from me, let his gaze travel jerkily over the bar.

'I'll have to do it myself, then.' He took a meditative sip of his beer. 'You're about as much good as a wet fish, Stubbs,' he said. He drained the rest of his glass, set it down on the table and wiped his lips. 'And I don't want to see you round by hers again,' he said. He stood up, nodded severely, and marched out through the door.

I sat there, finishing my beer more slowly, and went out into the streets; if I hurried I could get back to my pie-and-peas shop before it closed. There would be time enough to suffer when my stomach was less empty.

In fact, my stomach began to suffer directly it was full of pie-and-peas. My entrails, all my insides, had undergone awful contortions of coldness during the episode with Spaldine. Leaving the pie-and-peas shop, I had to make for the nearest public lavatory at the double.

It was one of those subterranean London affairs, and as I sank down on the seat in my stall, the subterranean nature of my life was borne in on me. My coming to the bloody capital was

meant as a great gesture of love; but so sub-
merged was everyone in the animal hurly-burly
of their lives that nobody had noticed it. Nobody.
Only my stomach, as it emptied, gave indications
that the gesture had ever been made.

All round me were other declarations of
abortive love. Beside the usual boastings about
length and frequency of climax and pleas for
assignation with eighteen-year-old R.A.F. boys,
several case histories were scrawled on the door
and walls. One was about a fellow luring a news-
girl into his kitchen on a Sunday morning and
sucking her off on the table. One began, 'My
older brother is in the Merchant Navy and when
he comes home he has to share my bed with
me.'

I read them with detached interest as I wiped
myself. Written large by my right-hand side was
a pencilled notice: 'Why Shit Here When There
Are Better Stories in the Next Cubicle?'

The story of my life, I thought.

My 'Virginia Journal' had travelled south
with me. Sitting on my bed and laying it on my
rickety little bedside table, I spent some hours
writing it up, trying to make sense of what was
happening.

There is some happiness now in seeing that

even then I was generous to Virginia, although I believed that society imposed a sort of obligation on me to judge her harshly and to hate her for her way of life: but that was a hangover from the kind of judgements exercised by a previous generation. Naive though my sentiments were, they ended with a sentence that now pleases me a lot: 'I never gave Virginia a single present (more poverty than meanness), and she never gave me one, but yet she gave me more than I can say.'

That was meant to be the last word.

I decided that Virginia wanted to see me no more than she did Spaldine; so I would fade out of her life. If that was her point of view, I had sympathy with it; we were in London now, not Branwells, and she no more wanted me in her bed than I wanted young Brown in mine; circumstances had altered cases. All this was pusillanimous, perhaps; it was not unnatural to feel down-hearted in the circumstances. I had no hatred of her—any hatred was directed towards the odious Spaldine.

Feeling extremely low, I brought out my comforter and commenced to rub it, gazing at it affectionately and thinking how ably it had worked to Virginia's and my mutual pleasure in that little nest of hers which she had never allowed me to see. It stood to attention at the thought. I began to grow enthusiastic myself. After the spasm of pleasure raked through my body I climbed into bed and went to sleep.

For the next day or two I went about pretending that a new phase in my life had begun. I cultivated a Miss Tregonin, a Cornish girl with a mass of freckles who was younger than I and also worked at the trestle table in the department. I had no intention of going home with my tail between my legs.

On Saturday came a letter from Virginia, written on her violet notepaper, saying that she was in trouble but would like to meet me at the National Gallery at noon that day. We could have lunch together.

'. . . in trouble *but* would like to see you . . .' Not '. . . in trouble *and* would like to meet you . . .' What was the distinction there, and was it one she had intended to make? What, for God's sake, was the trouble?

And the business about meeting her at noon. The department did not close until noon, so I could not hope to be at the National Gallery before 12.15. I pictured that frail little elusive figure among the columns; would it wait for me? Could it? What were the hidden pressures on its life that kept it moving all the while? I remembered what I knew intuitively: somehow, Virginia had been hurt.

So I slipped away from the department at 11.40, hoping nobody spotted me, and Virginia turned up at the Gallery at 12.30.

It happened that the Gallery was shut that day for what were euphemistically called 'Alterations'. Most of the pictures were being crated up and taken into the country. Trafalgar Square was a sober sight, with sandbags everywhere, and a great water tank, and other evidence of warlike preparedness. Like almost everyone else, Virginia and I carried our gas-masks in little square boxes.

We went and ate in a humble restaurant near Charing Cross Station. There were net curtains at the window, through which a wintry sun attempted to shine. We smiled at each other, hardly knowing what to say.

She made no attempt to apologise for the dreariness of our last meeting. Was she aware how miserable I had felt then? Rather sharply, I asked what sort of trouble she was in.

'You haven't the experience, Horry, to know how complicated life can be,' she began.

'I have more experience than you may believe, Virginia. I am no longer a kid, as I told you the other night.' Only a long while after did I realise that that declaration might not have the effect on her I intended. I was conscious then of my youth and of the fact that if she was in trouble then it was a man she needed; later I perceived that she could only achieve satisfactory relationships with boys—children, in fact, on whom her gentle, almost non-existent character could have some weight, and who might repose in her a trust she could not give herself.

She looked at me doubtfully, her head on one side. I was being judged in ways I could not know. 'I am sorry we are having to meet one another in London. It's all more complex than Branwells .... My life just is terribly complex. You can see how I have come down in the world, through no fault of my own. I'm such a silly about money matters, among other things. Now there's the war to make everything more difficult. I'm lucky to have such a good friend in Josie. . . .'

I took her hand and said, 'Virginia, darling, you also have a good friend in me. I'm not just another chap who screws you and disappears—I love you, I want to help you!'

'You mustn't use that ugly word, pet. You are a dear boy, but you can't help me.'

'How do you know? Tell me what sort of trouble you're in! I'm down here all on my own— I'm free to help in any way I can. I came to London just to help you. Of course, I'm a bit hard up. . . .'

The waitress arrived and we had to be quiet. We sat and looked at each other as the soup plates arrived. Then she said, 'I'm being watched night and day at Josie's place. It's her cousin— the one you saw. I know he is connected with the divorce in some way. They have got a man watching me, the solicitors. I believe he has a gun in his pocket.'

'Did he follow you here, to this restaurant?'

'I don't believe so. I went in and out of a few shops by different doors on my way to meet you. That's why I was slightly late.' So she had noticed she was late.

'Virginia, darling, I want to tell you something. I want you to understand that I do dearly love you. It's not just sexual attraction. I know all about the age difference between us, but it makes no difference to me—I love you just as you are. And I know more about you and your private life than you may think. It has no effect on my feelings for you.' I said that rather hastily, for a slight flicker of expression came over her face, a tiny change, something so transient—and then she directed her gaze down at the tablecloth.

The intuitive core in me felt her alter; but of course I overruled that and went on. 'It's true you are being watched, Virginia, but not for the reasons you imagine. You are being watched by Christopher Spaldine and he intends you no good. He has nothing to do with anyone in the house, but he wants to get revenge on you.'

Half-smiling, she said, 'Christopher Spaldine? He was one of the boys in the art club, wasn't he?'

'He was one of your lovers, Virginia!'

[176]

She kept looking at my shoulder with a fixed expression.

I babbled on, offering to guard her and I know not what else; but I had lost contact with her.

The meal was an absolute failure.

We paid the bill, half each at her insistence, and went outside. She was walking rather briskly, her short-cut fair hair bobbing, her head just slightly on one side. I held her arm. There were other people all round us; she could disappear.

'Come and spend the night with me, Virginia. Please—let me hold you in my arms, just as I used to do!'

I was terrified by the way she walked; she held herself stiffly and moved too fast. I manœuvred her into a stationer's shop and talked to her earnestly. She stood gently by me, picking at a thread on her coat, as I tried simultaneously to explain and discount the things Spaldine had told me.

Looking at me, smiling rather crookedly, Virginia said, 'We had better stop seeing each other, Horry, if you really believe those indecent things Christopher Spaldine said about me.'

That floored me. In the midst of my stammered explanations she said, 'Darling, I don't want to hurt you—you have been a dear boy. But if you are connected with all these other people, then I mustn't have any more to do with you.'

Her face was really rather hard and determined as she spoke.

All these other people. . . . Tears stood in my eyes in exasperation. I clutched her child-like body. Two assistants were standing behind the counter, grinning covertly and thoroughly enjoying our exhibition.

'Listen,' I hissed, for all the world like Spaldine himself. 'Come away! Leave everything! We'll go and live in another part of London. We'll get a little flat—I'll write to Father for money. You shall have no more worries, I swear. I'll never leave your side. We'll begin life again together!'

'I must go, Horry, I must go. You know I couldn't live with you if you are a friend of Spaldine's—I have evidence to prove he is in my cousin's pay.'

In her agitation she pushed from me and hurried from the shop. She was buttoning up her gloves as she went, and it was frightfully important they should be buttoned. I stood there for a moment, reeling. I knew it was hopeless. Then I had to follow or she would be gone for ever.

I passed the grinning assistants. 'Fuck off!' I said.

Virginia was walking slowly along the Strand. Unable to think what to say to her, I stayed a pace or two behind her. She turned left, down one of the side streets that lead to the Embankment. Perhaps she was going to throw herself in the Thames?

She started when I humbly touched her arm.

'Forgive me for upsetting you by anything I said, dearest Virginia! I hate Spaldine's guts—I told you, he attacked me, so he hates mine. Nor do I know any other single person in the world who knows you. Your past life is no business of mine, Virginia. I love you. Don't turn me away!'

'You're very sweet,' was all she said. We walked side by side silently. We stood looking at the Thames.

The intuitive core in me told me that she was seeking for ways to cast me off finally. I made an error then that I was to make again a few years later, more fatally. I begged her to marry me.

She stood there against me, her head down, as I grasped her arms through her thin coat—a ridiculous position, I suppose.

Finally, she looked up at me, with her face full of sweetness and gentleness. She said, 'What an amazing history we have had, Horry! You are a wonderful person and we have been like two children together, haven't we? But I have deeply misled you. Please don't be hurt. I've always warned you that life is much more complicated than you think. My own life is too involved for anyone else to contemplate. I already owe several thousand pounds to people—you could not shoulder such debts.'

'Are you telling me the truth?'

'It's all too true, I'm afraid. But I can't marry you for a different reason. I am already married. My husband was a terrible gambler, and I am saddled with his debts. . . .'

'You're married. . . .' It was as if I was drowning. No air reached my lungs.

'It was wrong of me not to tell you, darling, when you have been so sweet. Everyone who gets mixed up with me comes to grief.'

She lifted my hand and kissed it, glanced almost furtively at me, and then hurried off, walking with her quick light gait up the street we had come. I stood staring, my feelings curdling within me. She glanced back once before she disappeared. I started to cry, burying my eyes in my knuckles.

Was she married? Only a month before, I would have believed her had she told me she was a German spy. Now I did not know what to believe. If she said what she said just to shake me off, then her gambit was a success. I was beaten. There was nothing I could do for her; whichever way I turned, she would see my move as a hostile one, part of the plot against her. There was no room for truth in her world of lies.

How would you judge Virginia Traven? For years I made no attempt to pass judgement. She hurt me, but hurt seems intrinsic in human relationships, and the hurt was not her intention —in almost any situation, she was the injured party. As for her lies, they enriched and widened my narrow little world.

There remains the sexual aspect of the matter. How much harm did she do to the boys she seduced, to the boys with whom she so genteelly and discreetly lay? Speaking for myself, I was delighted to be seduced, I thirsted for it, I went to great pains to be seduced. The same would undoubtedly be true of the odious Spaldine and Angel-Face Knowles. Virginia was no harpy, devouring all who came along her path. She only took in those who sought her out, and there was nothing perverted in her actual love-making.

True, Spaldine was unbalanced by the affair; but I found some evidence, thinking back, that he was unbalanced long before Sister arrived at the school. He had run away from school once— one of only three boys who ever did so; that might seem like a sane act against the insanity of Branwells, but nobody who listened alertly to Spaldine would have regarded him as an apostle of reason.

And there was Knowles. Did he develop a mother-fixation through his thrilling association with Virginia? He became quite well known in later life as a mountaineer, and I read with curious insight in an illustrated magazine article that his wife was 'several years older' than he. Was that an attempt to relive the Virginia experience? I believe it much more likely that he was that way inclined long before, or why would he have been drawn to Virginia in the first place?

Virginia had powerful advantages over all the other girls I knew in those days, first among which was her experience. She was past the age of being embarrassed or of thinking of sex as a dirty joke. I was still at that age; so were my girl friends, like Esmeralda. Loving for Virginia, and consequently for her favoured boys, was a comforting and soothing thing. In her modest way she was expert; and expertise is really the butter on the bread of sex.

It is curious at last to write on the subject of Virginia. She passed out of my life twenty-eight years ago. Yet she has never been entirely absent from my life, even when I have not thought of her for months, perhaps years. Now I am on the subject, I can hardly bear to come off it.

I loved Virginia well. I did not love her for sex alone. Before I found out about all the lies, I believed her to be good, almost saintly. I can still see how and why I thought her so wonderful, although irrelevant things like snobbery clouded my judgement—for she must always have been no more prosperous than my family, and so the simple way she came into humble cafés with me was not the elegant piece of broad-mindedness I imagined it at the time, but the indifference of custom.

So I come back to my first intuitions about her —that she had been deeply hurt. Something in her childhood had disrupted the entire course of her life . . . such a judgement is a cliché now, so much so that it is often patronisingly dismissed by the sophisticated. But the elementary perception that childhood injustices warp lives has done little to affect the general consensus of opinion, which acts on an older and more primitive principle, that an eye merits an eye, that sin deserves punishment. In many cases it is the punishment which fathers the sin.

But I refuse to think of Virginia in these text-book terms. Something had severely hurt her in childhood—no doubt her nature was also prone to receive the hurt. As an adult, she would be classified now as paranoic, I suppose.

In my youthful eyes she was none of these things; she was only herself, a woman in whose arms I had first tasted beauty and release, and through them discovered my better self.

She left me standing by the Thames. It seemed to me that I would never be able to recover myself, that I had lost too much. After a little while it occurred to me to run after her, to seize her, to force her to believe me and tell the truth. But by then it was too late.

For the rest of the day I wandered through the city. The painful deflections of life that all the towns of Europe were suffering found their echo in England's capital. Barricades of sandbags were going up; the fountains were turned off in Trafalgar Square. A platoon of soldiers was marching towards Westminster; I stopped to watch them go by, looked at the set faces of the men, lacking individuality. Already children were being evacuated to the country. Their place was being taken by men in uniform.

Idly, I looked about to see if by any chance I could see Nelson. But it was my father I wanted. Perhaps he would come down to London and persuade me to go back home with him. . . .

The nights were closing in. As the sun went down, blackouts went up.

I had begun to relish my melancholy, but hunger overtook me. In those days I was always hungry. Half-lost, pretending I was wholly lost, I stopped on my way towards my favourite pie shop and drank a cup of tea at one of those wooden tea-stalls on wheels which stood in Leicester Square, enjoying being among the down-and-outs. Only when I had finished my pie-and-peas did initiative return to me.

Virginia had told me Josie's surname. With luck, I would find it in the phone directory, and her number. I could ring Virginia; the next day was Sunday. We could meet again. Somehow I could persuade her that I was no part of the conspiracy she imagined to be building against her. I would make her see I was innocent.

Back at Lou's, I borrowed her directory, found Josie's number, and put through the call. I knew Virginia hated talking on the telephone; perhaps she thought of it as a sinister instrument; but this was a case of necessity.

Josie answered. I recognised her languid voice immediately.

Without thought, I said, 'I have a present for Virginia. Tell her I must meet her at eleven o'clock tomorrow morning. She must meet me, because I am then leaving London almost immediately.' I named a church I had noticed near her house; church seemed a good canny idea.

It may have been the idea of a present; although I had never given her anything, I knew she would be childishly delighted by a present. As I was setting out to meet her that Sunday morning, I belatedly realised that I had indeed better take a present, just in case Virginia did turn up.

I had nothing to give her. I had no money with

which to buy her anything. For a moment, I contemplated stealing a piece of Lou's costume jewellery. Then I remembered that I had in my wallet the little silver holder to contain books of postage stamps which my mother had given me on my fifteenth birthday. The intention had always been to have my name engraved on it, but fortunately this had not been done. Virginia could have it.

Unthinkingly, I had chosen a time when a service was in progress in the church. Great sadness filled me as I stood by the wide deserted steps and looked across the faded prospect of Hyde Park, listening to the organ. In a way, I wanted this all to be a failure, wanted to lose Virginia, wanted everything to be spoilt and broken. That would be only just, and in tune with the dismal years that were past.

When I saw her coming I forgot all that and knew I had at least some strength to fight.

Such joy to see her again, worn and brave and small and half-nodding her greeting at me! I smiled and took her hand.

'We're late for the service, Virginia! Let's have a walk in the park!'

'Josie teased me and said it would do me good to go to church!'

'Perhaps it might do us both good. We'll try and make it next Sunday, shall we?'

'Horry, I did not expect to see you again after

what I told you yesterday. I can't spare much time now, only I didn't want you to be sad, so I came to see you.'

'I'm not sad, Virginia. There's something more I must say to you.'

'More even than you said yesterday?' She gave a painful smile.

We crossed the road and walked familiarly together, relieved for the moment not to have to talk.

When we were in the park she said, 'Darling, I should not have come. But I am frightened. To tell you the truth, I am getting a bit frightened to remain in the house. There is a man in the street watching me—it's not who you said it was, it's another man. I'm sure he has a big gun in his pocket. I'm afraid they are going to kill me.'

I just did not understand that she believed what she was saying. Trying to laugh it off, I said, 'You're making it all up, darling!'

Perhaps she also had thought about the whole situation over-night. Perhaps she saw, through the veil of all that obsessed her, that I was no part of the conspiracy against her. Perhaps she had struggled against herself, and won, and come to me to give me another chance. I don't know. But I should not have told her she was making it all up! By her expression, I knew I had committed a bad tactical blunder.

'You don't know my father! He's a dangerous

man! He would quite easily have my sister and me shot to inherit my grandfather's money.'

I blurted out, 'You haven't got a sister, Virginia!' Maybe I hoped shock therapy would work.

She began to walk on, talking rapidly, telling me I was getting involved in something I did not understand. Her gas-mask case rolled against her hip. Tagging by her side, I had to admit to myself that she was, after all, right; yesterday I had been innocent; today I was involved and no longer innocent. Perhaps she was correct to fear me because I was a part of her world, just as Britain had finally become involved in the far more squalid delusions of the man over in Berlin.

So I broke into what she was saying, and asked, 'Tell me just one thing—tell me if you said you were married simply to save me further hurt. You aren't really married, are you? I can't believe it!'

We stopped under a tree and looked at each other. Her grey uncertain eyes were searching my face. I believe she was not married; that would have been too binding a contract for her elusive nature; and possibly what she said next was the nearest she could come to an admission it was so. Lowering her head, she said five heavy words:

'He left me long ago.'

The words must have contained an inner truth —perhaps part of that secret truth of hers of which I had always been aware.

From a great distance I heard myself saying faintly, 'If you are free, Virginia, I will marry you.'

And from a great distance she replied, 'I shall never be free of him.'

They were words of farewell. I stood there, looking as she receded from me. I called to her, broke into a run, thrust my little silver token into her gloved hand. She walked on with it.

Circumnavigating bushes, dodging behind the park railings, I kept her in sight until her slight figure was obscured behind a building.

She walked off into the streets of London, those quiet grey Sunday streets, with her gas-mask swinging on her hip, and I never encountered her again. For a long while, when I had other girls, far more orthodox girls, when I was in uniform and they came and gaily went, I would recall Virginia—recall her dear lack of vividness with such vividness!—and fear for her in the double jungle: the real jungle of London and the equally real one that she had built in her own mind. For I understood by then how beyond help she was.